"Truce? _____ behind the door. A white rose poked through the opening.

Emma was so shocked she couldn't answer.

"I didn't have a white flag. Will this do?" When she didn't answer, he added, "I'm sorry."

"I'm sorry, too," she whispered at the same time.

He moved to her and took her in his arms, surrounding her with warmth, and comfort, and a protectiveness that surprised her. "Emma, I didn't stop to try and understand what you were feeling. I could only think how opposite we are. I didn't want to see the similarities. Pride is something I can understand. Believe me, I do."

Silence followed his admission. Then, "Why are you telling me this?" Emma asked.

"I need your understanding, Emma. You make me see something in myself I've never seen before. And I don't like myself very much."

"I like you," she whispered.

Her breath warmed his cheek, and he suddenly realized her arms had traveled around his waist. Her body pressed against his, her scent wreathed him with sensual awareness. His fingers slid into her hair while his thumbs stroked the contours of her lips. He felt the moment her breathing changed, felt the sharp thud of her heartbeat that echoed his own.

Their lips brushed in a promise of ecstasy that sent him reeling. . . .

WHAT ARE *LOVESWEPT* ROMANCES?

They are stories of true romance and touching emotion. We believe those two very important ingredients are constants in our highly sensual and very believable stories in the *LOVESWEPT* line. Our goal is to give you, the reader, stories of consistently high quality that may sometimes make you laugh, sometimes make you cry, but are always fresh and creative and contain many delightful surprises within their pages.

Most romance fans read an enormous number of books. Those they truly love, they keep. Others may be traded with friends and soon forgotten. We hope that each *LOVESWEPT* romance will be a treasure—a "keeper." We will always try to publish

LOVE STORIES YOU'LL NEVER FORGET
BY AUTHORS YOU'LL ALWAYS REMEMBER

The Editors

LOVESWEPT® • 340

Courtney Henke
Chameleon

 BANTAM BOOKS
NEW YORK · TORONTO · LONDON · SYDNEY · AUCKLAND

CHAMELEON

A Bantam Book / July 1989

LOVESWEPT® and the wave device are registered
trademarks of Bantam Books, a division of
Bantam Doubleday Dell Publishing Group, Inc.
Registered in U.S. Patent
and Trademark Office and elsewhere.

If you would be interested in receiving protective vinyl
covers for your Loveswept books, please write to this address
for information:

Loveswept
Bantam Books
P.O. Box 985
Hicksville, NY 11802

ISBN 0-553-22015-2

Published simultaneously in the United States and Canada

Bantam Books are published by Bantam Books, a division
of Bantam Doubleday Dell Publishing Group, Inc. Its trademark, consisting of the words "Bantam Books" and the
portrayal of a rooster, is Registered in U.S. Patent and
Trademark Office and in other countries. Marca Registrada.
Bantam Books, 666 Fifth Avenue, New York, New York 10103.

PRINTED IN THE UNITED STATES OF AMERICA

O   0 9 8 7 6 5 4 3 2 1

To Kathy, for letting me see the world through another set of eyes.

And to Tuesday nights. Thanks for everything.

One

Shoving wet brown hair from her forehead, Emma peered through the azaleas at Mr. Morgan's front steps, which appeared fuzzy in the waves of heat that rose from the adjacent driveway. Her cramped legs trembled from sustained crouching, but her patience, though sorely stretched, had suffered worse. Her mission was too important to let a little agony deter her. She had to leave St. Louis in less than eighteen hours, and she refused to slink home in defeat.

The setting sun threw shadows over the steps and she irritably shooed a bumblebee away from her ear as she strained toward a sound she sincerely hoped wasn't in her imagination. The lock rattled again, and Martha, Mr. Morgan's blue-haired secretary, exited his stately antebellum refuge. Emma's gray eyes narrowed on the woman she'd followed like a bloodhound, a rebel battle cry building in her throat. But she swallowed it, knowing she couldn't scare the support hose off the poor woman. At least, not yet.

Not until after she'd gotten inside the house.

Martha closed the door, then paused, a grimace of exasperation folding her already wrinkled features. Emma stiffened and ducked lower into the shrub, but Martha made no move toward her. Instead, she dug in her voluminous handbag, withdrew a key, unlocked the door, and stuck her head inside.

"Mr. Morgan!" she called. "Don't forget to call for the tickets to the charity ball!"

Emma thought she heard a sarcastic masculine voice yell "Thank you, Mother Martha!"

Martha chuckled and withdrew, closing the door behind her. The silver Cadillac Emma had followed earlier purred up the curved driveway. Martha stepped down to meet it. As her fingers touched the door handle, she frowned, as if sensing her audience, and darted a suspicious glance around the yard.

Emma froze and instinctively concentrated on the green of the leaves around her, feeling herself flow into its essence. Martha's gaze swept over her without pause. After a moment the woman shrugged and pulled open the car door, greeting the driver and obviously eager to answer some inaudible question. "No, Benno. If he'd let me help, it wouldn't be so hard on him. But in spite of his—"

To Emma's frustration, the rest of the provocative sentence was cut off by the slamming of the door. The limousine immediately rolled down into the street, taking Maxwell Morgan's guardian dragon away.

Now what, wondered Emma. She absently swatted a whining mosquito and mentally consigned the tax man to a burning pit for getting her into this situation in the first place. She threw Morgan in, too, for surrounding himself with overprotective employees.

Sighing, she peeled her blouse away from her lithe form. She had no right to blame anyone, especially the owner of Daniels Cosmetics, Maxwell Morgan. He hadn't even offered to buy her mother's fragrance, he'd merely sent them the least offensive rejection. It had been *her* bright idea to approach him personally without an appointment, *her* belief in a perfume that no corporate executive had given a chance. While the rest of her family stood arguing about what to do, Emma, as usual, had slipped away to do it.

Unconsciously she lifted her chin, sending coffee-color locks swinging around her shoulders. She would succeed, as she always did, because she had to. Her eyes zeroed in on the front door. Come hell or high water, she'd get in to see Maxwell Morgan, she vowed as she stood on wobbly legs.

Something snagged her panty hose, and she felt the tiny caress of a run as she made her way through the shrubbery, pulling her portfolio after her. She stumbled up the steps, and her ankle twisted beneath her. Wincing at both her nasty luck and a knife of pain, she lifted her foot. Her ankle burned when she touched it, but, when tested, it held her weight. With almost everything else going wrong, she was grateful she could still walk. But she would have to carry her shoes for a while, she decided as she kicked them off.

She raised her arm and knocked once on the door. For the first time in weeks the hard lines of stress disappeared, and her oval face smoothed into serene wonder as the door miraculously opened a few inches at the force of her knock. Emma couldn't believe her good luck. Apparently Martha hadn't pulled the door shut tightly enough to lock it.

Her confidence returned. She plucked azalea leaves from her hair, brushed a smudge of dirt from her suit jacket, and squared her shoulders. In her experience, people believed exactly what they saw. And Mr. Morgan would see such cool competence that he would buy with no reservations.

She gripped her briefcase and whispered the opening line that would hopefully pique his interest. "I'm here to offer you the deal of a lifetime. I'm here to offer you the deal . . ."

Chanting the words like a talisman, she limped inside quietly and glanced from one twilight-dim room to another. Only the drone of an air conditioner broke the almost stifling silence. Where was the man she had been chasing all day, she wondered as she peeked into the kitchen.

"What shall we do tonight, girl?"

Emma froze at the low, husky voice, panic sending her heartbeat racing. She darted guilty looks around the adjoining room, a casual living area, but saw nothing but shadows.

"Would you like me to read another chapter of that hot best seller to you? Or maybe we could go for a moonlight swim later. Would you like that?"

She gulped and caught herself before she answered yes. It was a voice any woman in her right mind would dream of hearing late at night, whispering endearments in the dark. But when a strange, moaning sigh answered him, floating through an arched doorway to her right, Emma's palms began to sweat. If Mr. Morgan had female company, he would hardly want to listen to a sales pitch. Groaning inwardly, knowing she had no options left, Emma approached the doorway. This was it, she told herself. This was the biggest gamble of her life. She couldn't stop herself from crossing her fingers behind her as she paced silently to the threshold.

The library was dim, and she paused, letting her eyes adjust. The faint odor of leather and mildew told her the owner had expensive tastes, but she had no time to examine the room. She saw only one occupant, and every other thought flew out of her mind.

He lounged in a big leather chair, his head

back, half-lidded eyes focused somewhere on the ceiling. His hair was pure gold, all a-tumble, with one wayward lock hanging over his eyebrows. He wore no shirt, and the setting sun sent intriguing shadows dancing over a wide chest littered with darker hair. Any of the seven other women in her family would have drooled over the masculine feast before them, but Emma found herself staring at his face.

She'd seen only one picture of him in her research, in the fiscal report just after he'd inherited Daniels Cosmetics six years earlier. That quietly determined twenty-eight-year-old had not changed into the hardened misanthropic executive she'd expected to be cynical beyond his years. He'd metamorphosed into a man who would laugh in the face of demons! Humor lurked in the corners of his mouth, as if the entire world silently amused him, and that disturbed her because she could not figure out why *this* man surrounded himself with a battalion of staff members intent on keeping people away. To a woman who'd lived most of her life staring yearningly at the horizon, dreaming of faraway places, he was impossible to understand. Why would he hide himself away? What secrets did he conceal?

He frowned suddenly, as if in pain, and lifted a hand to rub a whitened, jagged scar just under his hairline. His fist clenched on the desk. Something inside Emma twisted, and she felt the most amazing urge to wrap him in her arms. But she couldn't, could she? She was an intruder, and she was uncomfortably aware that she had witnessed a man with his guard down. Guilt flooded her, and her honor demanded that she go out and give warning before she entered again.

As she began to inch away, a low growl rumbled from somewhere in the room. Instantly the man stiffened.

"What is it, Dixie?"

A dog! she thought. She wouldn't have time to ease into this now, and she tensed, knowing she already had one strike against her. If only she hadn't come up with this harebrained idea!

His head turned as he crooned to the unseen Dixie.

Instinct took over. Emma melted into the shadows. His gaze swept the room, but there was no sign that he acknowledged her presence, and she easily swallowed her panic. Those eyes! The light was failing, but she could see their amber glint, several shades darker than his hair. Maxwell Morgan was one fine specimen of a man!

"It's okay, girl. Another mouse, huh?"

Emma nearly sighed in relief. She had a second chance. This time she wouldn't blow it by sneaking into his—

With a suddenness that startled her, Maxwell Morgan threw his head up, his nostrils flaring like a great golden palomino testing the wind.

Think fast, Emma.

What was that incredible scent, Max wondered in awe. Fresh, clean, faintly sweet, it transported him to a high cliff swept by sea breezes that carried the faraway fragrance of island flowers. A natural blend, he knew. No chemicals could do it justice. Primary . . . jasmine, he thought. Secondary . . . sweet flag? Tertiary . . . oh, hell. This was something to be experienced, not analyzed. He detected the subtle aroma of budding flowers and spring grasses, honeyed somehow. Yet it held the sultry quality of some unknown hothouse flower.

He frowned, wondering from where in heaven that scent had drifted. With his company's reputation for developing unusual perfumes, they could make millions. The scent would hit the market like wildfire, but—

The hair on the nape of his neck stood rigid.

Dixie's aging sense of hearing hadn't been wrong. There *was* someone in the room, someone other than Benno or Martha. But Dixie obviously hadn't seen anyone yet, which gave him a possible clue to the intruder's whereabouts.

"Step out of the shadows, whoever you are!" he called in his most commanding tone. "Or I let the dog loose!"

"No, please, Mr. Morgan! I'm not a thief! I'm here to—to offer you the life of a dealtime!"

Silence hung quivering in the room after the panicky pronouncement, and Max didn't know whether to bellow, call the police, or laugh. Before he could decide, the female voice went on. "Damnation! My tongue wrapped around my eyeteeth, and I couldn't see what I was sayin'."

"That sounds painful," he couldn't help replying.

"Lord, you have a sense of humor." She chuckled, a low, husky sound that sent shivers up his spine. "Mr. Morgan, you're not going to believe this, but I'm not in the habit of housebreaking. It's just—I've been followin' your people around all day, hoping to catch you. I'm fryin' in this suit, I'm tired, and I feel like a royal ass for entering your lovely home uninvited." She drew a deep breath. "If I walk away and come in as if you'd never seen me, I promise to walk the straight and narrow from now on, all right?"

Max gaped, his head spinning as he tried to sort through her request.

"Thank you," she said on a sigh, then thudded away in an off-rhythm pace, muttering to herself. "He's got you so flustered, you don't know which end is up anymore. You can't even get the words out of your mouth. Bloody stupid twit, look at yourself! Better strip off these panty hose before . . ."

Her voice trailed off in the distance, and Max shook his head sharply. "What in the hell was that?" he murmured.

Dixie licked his hand and curled up at his feet.

Either that incredibly sensuous female had been his imagination, or else Dixie sensed the whirlwind had been no threat.

To his surprise, he preferred to trust Dixie's instincts. His curiosity was stronger than any fear he might have felt. The woman had the audacity of a hurricane, whoever she was, and she appealed to his sense of the absurd. Anyone with that much brass deserved something for her effort.

And her voice intrigued him in spite of himself. Her smooth southern drawl held a delightful trace of a British accent, which had immediately captured his interest. She sounded like a wanton and smelled like a summer breeze. But what did she want?

Had she said something about panty hose?

Every square inch of his body tightened with the erotic image she'd evoked. He gulped, fighting his disconcerting arousal. He couldn't remember anyone ever having this sudden effect on him, and he wasn't sure he liked it. She'd walked right into his house, for heaven's sake! And who knew how long she'd stood there watching him!

Resentment stirred. This was his home, his sanctuary, and she had assumed total control of the situation. That was something he could not allow.

A whisper of sound, a whiff of her delectable fragrance, alerted him to her return. "Who are you?" he asked without preamble.

"My name is Emma Machlen, and I'm here to offer you the deal of a lifetime."

Max caught the reluctant, admiring grin before it could reach his mouth. Gone was the flustered southern dynamo of a moment before. In her place stood a calm saleswoman, radiating confidence. Unfortunately he recognized her name. "Machlen? From Organic Island Industries? Your company wrote to me a month ago about a scent made with some grass I'd never heard of?"

"Yes."

He heard a trace of wariness in her tone and felt honestly sorry that he'd have to burst her bubble. "As I told you in my letter, I don't buy fragrances developed outside my own company."

"All I want is five minutes of your time to change your mind."

"You won't."

She sighed. "Mr. Morgan, I'm truly sorry that I approached you in this manner, all grimy and everything, but all I'm asking for is a chance."

He frowned, recalling her comment about dirt. She really thought her looks would affect his decision! That tickled his wry sense of humor and gave him the edge his mind needed. "Ms. Machlen, I can honestly say that I didn't notice your appearance."

"Very gallant, sir. I knew you were a gentleman from your letter."

"Don't depend on it," he muttered, and steepled his fingers underneath his chin. She was growing more and more fascinating every moment. "How did you get in?"

"Through the front door. You really should have that latch checked," she said sternly. "Anything could crawl in."

"No," he scoffed. "By any chance, are you wearing the fragrance you're offering?"

"Yes," she said in relief.

He rubbed his lower lip with the side of his finger. The fact that the scent was made from rare grass had quelled his initial excitement but hadn't killed his interest. Several things could complicate mass production, he realized, least of which was whether or not she wore a duplicatable formula or a fluke used only to sell him. One question immediately rose to mind. "Why doesn't your company produce it?"

She hesitated. "We're a cottage industry, Mr. Morgan. Unfortunately at the moment we have neither the equipment nor the distribution system to do it the justice it deserves. You have."

A tiny quiver in her voice told him that there was more to it than that. "What else?"

"I—I beg your pardon?"

"You could wait until you were capable of producing it yourself, Ms. Machlen. Why sell if it's so good?"

"We need immediate liquid capital, Mr. Morgan. For . . . another project."

He would be a fool to buy a pig in a poke, especially from this woman. She'd invaded his house, disturbed him in more ways than one.

But he'd never turned away someone in need, though why he was convinced of that in spite of her plausible explanation, he didn't know. And if this grass was available in quantity, and if she could prove that the formula could be repeated . . .

"You have your five minutes, Ms. Machlen."

Emma couldn't hide her relief at his statement. She had her chance! Immediately she calmed herself. This was business, and she'd already almost made a complete mess of it. She had her foot in the door; now it was up to her to do the rest.

Consigning her rumpled clothes to the back of her mind right beside her attraction to him, she snatched her portfolio off the floor and began to pull out her carefully drawn illustrations for her presentation. She looked around the room and for the first time noticed how precisely his furniture stood. The line of stereo and computer equipment that nearly spanned one wall was the only light source. The sun had set while they'd talked, yet he'd made no move to turn on the overhead lamp.

She limped to the switch on the wall beside the kitchen door. "May I?"

He waved his hand, a tiny smile playing across his beautifully shaped mouth. She gulped and stifled the urge to kiss those lips. Business, she told herself firmly as she flipped on the light and returned to her sketches. Sell him. You can do it, Emma. Think high-powered executive.

Her treacherous body warmed all over, mocking her pep talk. She ignored it, just as she ignored her blurred and gritty eyes. She couldn't afford it.

"Mr. Morgan, we were impressed with your company from the very beginning. Though Daniels Cosmetics is small, Dancer made you one of the top competitors in a fierce market. Packaging sells the product, but you've managed to create a reputation for unique fragrances unequaled in the industry. All of your perfumes are unusual and arresting."

She heard him chuckle and winced at her choice of words. The man unnerved her. It was as if he could see right through her brave facade. That had never happened before. She was too good at creating her illusions.

Hands trembling, she forced her odd emotions down deep inside her and concentrated on propping her design on the chair placed neatly in front of his meticulous desk. "In—in short, Mr. Morgan, you are in the ideal position to make a fortune from a scent that not only changes with each woman"—she paused for effect—"but with her moods as well."

She turned and smiled at him, but instead of being suitably impressed, Mr. Morgan seemed to be only politely listening. Even his gorgeous eyes were unfocused, as if he'd lost interest. Her heart sank even as her determination rose. For some reason she wanted his good opinion whether he bought the scent or not. He was an intriguing man, but he sure was one tough customer.

Well, she'd never thought it would be easy. But cold sweat broke out on her brow as she stared at the first drawing, a pastel rendering of a dreamy-eyed woman surrounded by several images, all focusing on an embrace with a strong male figure. Her niece, Catherine, had done her usual exquisite work, and Emma's pride cloaked her nervousness.

"Though the grass is used in small quantity, it responds to a woman's slightest change in body chemistry. Mr. Morgan, this is the fragrance that will revolutionize the industry." Her voice built to a crescendo. "This is the scent that will never go out of fashion."

She gestured grandly. "Introducing Chameleon. For the woman who dares to become her fantasy."

"Ms. Machlen," he said quietly.

Emma halted, suddenly feeling awkward, as if she'd made some huge error. But she hadn't! Why wouldn't he give her a chance to finish?

She hastily shuffled to the next drawing. "A special fragrance deserves a unique bottle. The crystal figure on the stopper and the shape itself will—"

He cleared his throat, and she saw to her dismay that he'd lost his smile. "Ms. Machlen, I've let this go on far too long. I'm sorry, but I—I don't think you've researched your market as carefully as you thought you had."

"But—" All her long hours, the days of racking her brain for this concept, all the sleepless nights preparing herself for this moment, seemed to be spinning down the drain. She hadn't done anything wrong! She couldn't fail! Her mouth firmed. "Mr. Morgan—"

"You don't understand. I can't—"

The clatter of the computer cut him off.

"Excuse me," he said, and stood to turn toward his printers.

Printers? she saw with a frown. Two of them? Why would anyone need two?

He bent over the printout, running his hands

lightly over the page like a child who couldn't keep his place.

But that made no sense. He was obviously a well-educated man. Why—

All the blood drained from Emma's face, leaving her woozy. "Oh, Lord," she whispered, and grabbed the edge of his desk as if her life depended on it. No wonder her designs hadn't impressed him.

Maxwell Morgan was blind.

Two

"It's not important," Max said. "A little technical problem."

Emma stared at him blankly. *Not important?* she thought. That this man would never see the world as she yearned to do? That she had spent three days frantically putting together a worthless presentation? That for once appearances had deceived her instead of the other way around?

That he would never be fooled by her camouflage?

A giggle built, and she clamped her hand over her mouth to prevent its escape. She had thought he couldn't see her because she didn't want to be seen! She'd never understood why it worked, just that it always had. And he thought *he* had a little technical problem?

Laughter bubbled forth like pure spring water, washing away knots of tension she hadn't even known existed.

"Ms. Machlen?"

Emma glanced up to find Max standing beside his desk, dressed in nothing but jeans, a quizzical half smile tilting his full mouth. He couldn't possibly understand the absurdity of the situation!

"I've never had quite this reaction before," he said dryly. "You figured it out, huh?"

"Oh, yes." Giggling, Emma sank to the chair opposite her precious, useless drawings. "Hoisted by my own petard."

"I wouldn't quite say that."

"You would if you knew."

"Knew what?"

"If I told you, you'd think I was bonkers."

"I thought that was a given," he said blandly.

"Maybe so," she said, her laughter slowing. Her body warmed all over at his smile. She cleared her throat. "If—if you want to know the truth, I'm relieved."

"Relieved?"

"I—I thought—"

"Herr Morgan?"

At the sound of the unfamiliar voice, Emma swallowed her amusement. A stocky man entered the room, hat in hand. That figurative veil of hers swirled into place.

"Herr Morgan? I knocked, but you did not answer, and Martha swore someone was lurking in the bushes, though she saw no one."

"I'm fine, Benno." Max grinned. "Monday I want a new alarm system, though."

At the sound of a muffled snicker, Benno whirled in surprise. His jaw dropped. "I—I'm—am I interrupting—"

"Just business, Benno."

Benno gaped nonetheless, thinking that business should have been the last thing on Herr Morgan's mind. The woman reminded him of the tiny oval portraits he had seen in an antique shop in Ladue. Her delicate features and wide round eyes held the natural beauty of another era, a stunning quality that had nothing to do with makeup. Her shoulder-length brown hair and tan suit did nothing to exaggerate her slender curves, but flattered them nonetheless. This lady didn't need artifice; she glowed from within.

At complete odds with her docile posture, she

seemed to be fighting a laughter that made her eyes gleam with tears, her mouth dimple. *Ach!* If he were forty years younger . . .

" *'N Abend, Fraulein.*"

" *'N Abend.*"

He brightened. *"Sprechen sie Deutsch?"*

"Ich spreche etwas Deutsch."

Her accent was perfect, he thought, and straightened. "If you'll need nothing else, Herr Morgan."

"Ms. Machlen, do you have a car?"

Emma nodded, dazed by Benno's scrutiny, something she wasn't used to allowing. Then she realized the futility of her nod, and her shoulders shook. "Yes, I do." She had planned on doing some sight-seeing. *"Danke,* Herr Morgan," she couldn't resist adding impishly.

"Bitte," he said with a smile. "Go on, Benno. I shouldn't need you until it's time to pick up Adam at the airport on Monday."

"Yes, sir." He bowed to Emma, a quaint gesture she found endearing, and he left through a sliding glass door in the back of the room.

Max locked it, returned to his desk, and perched on its edge, crossing his arms in front of him. "Now, suppose you tell me why you're relieved."

She couldn't tell him all of it. He already thought she was crazy. "I, uh, thought you were bored."

"I've been a lot of things in the last few minutes, but bored wasn't one of them."

His voice sounded so strange that Emma's breath caught in her throat. The words tied her up in knots, making her hands tremble nervously. Could he possibly have fought the same strange emotions she had?

Not this man. She had the feeling that whatever battles he fought, he won. But his face looked familiar at that moment. Not the features, but the stern expression that seemed forced. Emma giggled. "You look just like old Mr. Wyler."

"Who?"

"My high school principal. On the day I filled his office with balloons."

He gave up and grinned. "Now, why do I have the feeling you did that sort of thing often?"

"I don't know. Why?"

"Do you always find everything so amusing?"

"Don't you?"

He cocked his head. "Sometimes. I just don't get caught."

"Neither do I. Usually."

He leaned forward, and she caught a whiff of his masculine scent. "Aren't you worried that I might have you arrested?"

Jail was the last thing on her mind. "If you ain't want to dead, don't born," she muttered.

"What was that? West Indian?"

"Gullah. More or less."

"You have a wealth of colorful sayings, don't you? I know I'm going to hate myself in the morning, but what does it mean?"

"It basically means if you aren't willing to face the consequences, don't take chances."

He stiffened. "And you take a lot of chances."

"Not really." His obvious disapproval confused her. "But if you're alive, you're already playing the biggest lottery of them all." And the chance she wanted to take at the moment astonished her.

She swallowed convulsively, her laughter fleeing in the wake of realization. He sat so close that their knees almost touched. The warmth from his body seemed to reach out, to cloak her and create a safer haven than she could ever do on her own. It was as if because he couldn't see her, she wanted him to, and the paradox confounded her. She had given him a glimpse of her inner self, something few people ever saw. And she had the oddest feeling he would be able to see inside her whether she let him or not.

Her pulse raced as she gazed into his tawny, sightless eyes. They were the windows to the soul, her mother always said. But his were a one-way mirror, as empty and emotionless as a desert summer. Because they always were? Or because he wanted them to be? "You have the most beautiful eyes," she said. "It's a shame—"

He clenched his fist. "What?"

"That you let them be so cold."

Max's head spun. The spell this woman had woven with her contagious laughter had suddenly taken on a dimension he didn't understand. Her evocative voice throbbed with a poignant emotion, one he knew wasn't pity. Blood roared in his ears. "I don't."

"You do, and I don't know why."

He swore he felt her breath on his cheek, and shivered, feeling completely naked to her in a way he'd never been before. He smelled the subtle change in her fragrance, which brought to mind an image of bodies tangled together in the ultimate kind of intimacy, of mutual pleasure, of secrets whispered in the dark. Of glory.

He leapt to his feet, forcing his hands to his side when they wanted to reach out and touch her. He wouldn't let her confuse him. He needed distance. "I'm going to put on a shirt," he said stiffly.

"And—and my proposal."

"Leave it. My colleague and I will look it over on Monday."

"That's too late!" Emma cried before she could stop herself. "I mean—" She bit her lip, wondering what in the world had possessed her. Why had she begun this conversation? Everything depended on her ability to sell the perfume to him, not to psychoanalyze him!

"You'll stay for dinner," he commanded, emotion flickering in the tawny depths of his eyes just for a moment. He opened his mouth to say something more, then closed it, and strode past her, out the door. "Dixie, come."

A huge golden retriever got up from beneath the desk, startling Emma, who had forgotten its existence. It glanced her way, as if taking stock of her, then paced slowly out after its master.

Emma breathed deeply of the scent left in Max's wake, his own personal, purely masculine fragrance. She couldn't move, couldn't think, couldn't seem to focus on anything but the emptiness of the room now that he was gone.

The sound of his rapid footsteps on the stairs echoed through her like a sledgehammer, bringing her back to reality. She'd just bared her soul, yet he'd shrugged her off like one of the whining mosquitoes outside. And she'd allowed it! Lord, she'd *helped* him forget her proposal! What had she been thinking, talking of high school and his personal life, which had absolutely nothing to do with the subject at hand?

He'd ordered her to dinner. Something inside her bristled at his egotistical assumption, his arrogant tone. Heaven only knew she'd heard it often enough in her life, from her parents, her siblings, her fiancé.

Who in the seven pits of Hades did he think he was?

Her spine stiffened, and she turned, staring at the empty doorway with narrowed eyes. "Oh, no, I won't stay for dinner with you, you—you—"

Frustrated, she threw herself back in her chair, burying her fingers in her sweat-dampened hair. She had to stay. Time was running out, and she had no options left. It was the only chance she'd have to explain her campaign.

After all, she told herself firmly, that's why she was there. To sell a perfume. She couldn't allow herself to become tied up in knots over a man who'd erected walls thicker than Jericho's around himself, a man who was so lonely that he invited strange women to dinner.

She frowned. Lonely? Why had that word popped

into her mind? It was hardly a concept she would have applied to him. He seemed so . . . self-contained.

But his voice haunted her. She had a sudden aching wish that she could play the trumpet, to make those walls come a-tumblin' down.

Emma slumped in the chair, physically and emotionally drained. Two sleepless nights and a harrowing day had finally caught up with her, and this horrible, unfamiliar feeling of defeat didn't help. If she were home, she'd crawl into her bed and sleep like a corpse, she knew. Nothing could rouse her when she was this tired. *Arouse* her, maybe, she thought disgustedly. One certain person could do that more easily than she cared to admit.

She sighed and rubbed her forehead in an unconscious imitation of Max's gesture, then stood, groaning when she saw the drawings. Catherine had spent hours on them, and they were about as useful as a three-legged horse.

Aching muscles demanded relief, and she rolled her shoulders back, wondering how she could salvage the situation. Could she just tell him about it, describe everything in such detail that his imagination would create its image? The drawings, maybe, but. . .

She shook her head helplessly. She needed something better. Even her written proposal was useless. She plopped the neatly typed pages on top of the sketches. Then her gaze flitted to his braille printer.

Her gray eyes narrowed, an idea forming in her mind. If she had a three-dimensional drawing, Max could see the unusual bottle.

"That's it!" she cried. Revitalized, her mind worked quickly. A glance at her watch told her it wasn't too late, that the stores should still be open. She had to change into her jeans, probably in the car or a gas station restroom. But she wouldn't be able to stay for dinner.

She was surprised how much that realization disappointed her.

"That was adolescent," Max told himself for the thousandth time as he splashed cold water on his cheeks to cool his reaction to her. He started out the bathroom door, then paused and scrubbed his face with a towel before following the wall into his bedroom. "You had to show off, didn't you? You could have killed yourself, running up those damned stairs." He rubbed the scar on his forehead and slammed open the door. "Acting like you were a kid. A sighted kid, yet!"

And he'd invited her to dinner! He forced his mind away from his reasons, his disturbing lack of self-discipline around the woman downstairs, and concentrated on the present.

The layout of the familiar room hovered in his mind. The huge built-in closet to his left, the king-size bed with the heavy, shelved headboard just ahead, the rowing machine on the floor to his right. They flickered before him, a crystal-clear picture of reality. But it wasn't real, and trembling mentally, he banished the illusion.

Instead, he let his mind drift back to his childhood, the times he had pounded up those same stairs only to zip down the banister, much to the dismay of his mother. The polished mahogany floor had nearly broken his tailbone hundreds of times. It was still in his mind's eye, the rainbow-colored pattern the late afternoon sun used to make through the stained glass of the door. It had been his favorite game, to see if he could land on that patch of the rainbow.

Well, he thought without humor, that door was gone. He had put his fist through the rainbow the day they'd told him his blindness was permanent. Five years seemed like a lifetime ago.

Max ruthlessly stamped down any bitterness, as he always did. He accepted himself the way he was, just as he had accepted his parents' deaths, just as he had accepted his girlfriend's desertion after the accident that had cost him his sight. Emma Machlen was wrong, he thought. Life wasn't a lottery, it was a poker game. You were dealt your cards, but it took skill to make them work, to come out the big winner. And sometimes it was smarter to stack the deck.

Yet for the first time in years he felt like playing a questionable hand. What was it about Emma that brought out that old streak of recklessness? Women came and went in his life all the time. Why was she different?

He shook himself, knowing he could think in circles before he understood any of it. He didn't need anyone, especially someone who'd managed to make him act completely out of character at every turn.

He focused on her business proposal, on the bewitching fragrance that had enticed him to step out of his reserve, even if for a moment. That's what it was, he told himself. Her perfume. It had absolutely nothing to do with getting personally involved with Emma Machlen. It had nothing to do with her throaty, evocative voice, one that slipped into German or Gullah. It had nothing to do with an underlying sensuality that hovered between them like a steamy Louisiana summer.

"It's just business," he murmured, and reached to his drawer for a shirt, checking the braille color code automatically. Socks were in the next drawer, all meticulously arranged and sorted by Benno. His briefs weren't coded, but Benno could be trusted not to peek to see if they matched his shirt.

Would Emma peek, he wondered with a strange, fleeting ache.

"Now, that," he muttered, "is really adolescent."

After dressing, Max called Dixie and worked his way down the stairs, his traitorous mind giving him an uncomfortably voluptuous image of Emma Machlen. He missed a step, caught himself, and cursed silently as he strove to concentrate on where he was going.

"Mr. Morgan?"

Max froze, praying she hadn't seen him trip. "What?"

"I'm sorry, but I can't stay for dinner. I—I have things to do."

"But—" He cut himself off, squaring his shoulders. He would not reveal how much he wanted her to stay. "Fine."

"Don't look so relieved. Sherman had it easier than you!"

He heard her swish away like a breeze, heard the door open and close, and he gripped the banister painfully. Silence settled once more in his home, the peace he had fought for all his life. No one telling him what he should do, what he should be, how he should think. No one turning every situation around to his or her benefit. No one threatening his control.

The big, empty house had never felt so hollow. It was as if someone had sucked the life out of it.

"Come on, Dixie," he called, forcing a hearty tone he was far from feeling. "Let's have that dinner." He swallowed a tight knot in his throat and whispered, "We have the place all to ourselves."

Max paused in the library early the next morning, rebelting his robe, his senses fully awake. Her perfume lingered in the air. He allowed himself one unguarded moment to dream, then scoffed at his foolishness. His muscles shrieked from his late, frenetic session on the rowing machine, but he ignored their protest. His gut wrenched as he thought of her gentle voice, caressing him like fingers, and he mentally shoved the thought away.

But there was something he couldn't shake off.

"This is stupid," he told the faithful Dixie as she snuffled his hand. "She left. She walked right out without a backward glance." He smiled sadly. "At least, I think she did."

Dixie whined, as if trying to tell him something. "You can't possibly miss her. The woman is a lunatic! She broke into our house!" And stole his peace.

He sighed and moved into the kitchen. His questing hands found the familiar items, and he measured the water, poured it into the coffee maker, and slid the paper filter into the basket.

As he absently pulled out the coffee can and began to scoop the grains, he finally identified the pang of emotion he felt—the same pang he'd felt when she hadn't come back the night before. Disappointment. She'd given up too easily. Somehow he'd thought she was a fighter, yet she had walked out without even trying to convince him to buy her perfume.

As he moved around the kitchen seeking cooking utensils, something tugged at his distracted mind. He paused. Where was the smell of coffee? His hands told him the carafe was hot, very hot, but . . .

Max pulled out the basket. It was empty! When he discovered the small pile of grounds on the counter, he hung his head and chuckled, knowing he'd deposited them beside the basket.

After making the coffee, he decided to take a swim. His entire Saturday stretched before him like a dusty country road.

His jaw firmed. He would not let one woman defeat him. Instead of feeling sorry for himself, wishing she hadn't left, he would grab his tape recorder from his desk and work until he dropped. Martha would have a heart attack on Monday when she found a pile of dictation.

Once in the library, he reached into his top drawer for the recorder—and froze.

"No, Danny, I want . . ." The rest of the slurred phrase trailed off into a mumble.

His heart seemed to leap in his chest. It couldn't be! "Emma?" he called softly, but there was no answer. The voice seemed to have come from the computer. He moved toward it, stepping on an unfamiliar object. A wallet, his fingers told him, but it wasn't his. He placed it on his desk and turned, stubbing his toe painfully on an out-of-place chair. Someone was definitely there.

Then he found her.

She was slumped over the keyboard, her head not quite resting on the pillow of one arm, the other arm trailing down. His light touch roused her slightly, and she mumbled again before her breathing evened out.

When did she come back, he wondered, and ran his fingers over the braille printout. "Good Lord," he whispered. She'd redone her entire proposal! A jacket had been draped over the printer to muffle its loud clacking. Next to it rested a piece of clay shaped into what seemed to be her unusual bottle design. She'd even created a box with a raised picture on it. Emma must have been up all night!

He swallowed, but the lump in his throat refused to dissolve. He'd been right about her. She was a determined woman.

His hands returned to her almost against his will. Her hair was a mess, he noted with an odd twist in his gut, but it was so very, very soft. His fingers pressed closer as he knelt beside her, rippling its thick mass like a stone does the surface of a pond. He wondered fleetingly if it was the color of corn silk, since it had the feel.

His thumb traced the outline of her lips. They were full and velvet-soft, and he couldn't resist their lure. He leaned close and pressed his mouth against hers. She sighed in her sleep, her breath warm and moist on his lips. Her fragrance wrapped him in a calm sea that quickly became stormy. Fire shot through his loins.

Gasping, he jerked back and rubbed his palms down his robe, but the rough terry cloth couldn't erase the feel of her.

"Ms. Machlen?" he called, then louder, "Emma!"

She mumbled something that sounded like "Not a shadow, Danny." Max sighed and reached out to what he hoped was her shoulder. It was, he noted with relief, and he shook it gently. Then he pulled his hand back, but not before her satin skin had seared his senses. Nothing but a thin strap had covered it. "Ms. Machlen?" His voice cracked, but she stirred. "Wake up."

"Mmm . . ." Her groan sent shivers up his spine, then she hissed in pain, and his concern overrode anything else. He dropped to his knees beside her and reached out to touch her.

"What's wrong, Emma?"

"I hurt," she said, sobbing. She groaned again, and he felt the muscles tense under his hand. Sliding both hands to her neck, he buried his fingers in her hair and supported her head. His thumbs cradled her cheeks, and he felt the rectangular indentation of the keyboard on one of them.

His heart twisted, and he began to rub the tight muscles of her neck. "Why did you do this to yourself, you little idiot?" he whispered, surprised by the catch in his voice. "You could have asked me. I could have helped you. Why are you so desperate?"

She whimpered. He eased the pressure of his fingers, his emotions jumbled inside of him. "And why are you doing this to me?" He moaned and rested his forehead on her for a moment, then pulled back sharply. "Dammit, I don't want you here, lady! You disrupt my life!"

"Sssorry," she said, breathless.

He hesitated but continued the massage, feeling his anger flow away as her knots unwound. "You are the most exasperating woman I've ever known."

"Runs in the family."

He chuckled, and his strokes became softer.

She sighed. "Thank you, Max," she whispered.

"For what?"

"'F' chasing him away."

Max frowned. "Who? Danny? Is he your brother?"

She gave a halfhearted, unladylike snort. "Hardly. Fiancé."

The world spun under his knees. "You're engaged?"

"Not anymore." A single tear rolled to his thumb. "He never listened to me. Always . . ." She yawned, and her voice trailed off. "Always wanted everything his way . . . Like everybody else . . . You always . . ."

His breath caught. "He's gone now, honey. Don't worry."

"So sleepy," she mumbled, and he heard her breathing even out.

He shook her. "Emma, you can't sleep here. Don't you have a hotel to go to?" No answer. She couldn't drive in this condition anyway, he rationalized. "Come on, Emma, I'll take you to bed." He gulped. "I mean, to the guest room."

"Jus' a minute, Mama. So tired . . ."

"Emma." He shook her again. "Emma!"

" 'Cept the consequences," she muttered. "Max, I did it again. Nobody had the right kind of printer. Am I goin' to jail?"

"No, honey. I couldn't send you to jail."

She sighed and snuggled into him. "And you'll be able to see my pr'posal now, hmmm?"

He gasped as his manhood surged against his robe. If she only knew how much his mind was letting him see. "Yes, Emma. I'll look it over in a minute."

"You have to buy it, 'cause . . ."

"Why, Emma? Why do I have to buy it?"

She yawned. "Wanna go to bed."

Good Lord, he had to control himself. She wasn't even awake! All he could think about was her in his bed, not the one in the guest room. "Then stand up." He stood and raised her to her feet. She swayed under his hands. She was taller than he thought she'd be but so fragile. "Come on, Emma. You have to walk."

"I can walk by myself."

Her knees immediately buckled, and he grabbed her shoulders. "You have to help me, honey. I can't carry you." Visions of him tripping on the stairs with her in his arms brought the panic he hated. "Emma! Do you hear me? You have to walk."

" 'Kay."

Trustingly she pulled away, and her hand nestled in his. He swallowed convulsively, then squared his shoulders and led her toward the door. "Talk about the blind leading the blind," he muttered, but managed to lead her up the stairs at a snail's pace without incident. "Here's your door, Emma. Go get some sleep." As he heard the lock rattle and her door open, he turned away in relief.

"I can disappear," she said suddenly, clearly.

"Just not from my house," he muttered.

She yawned. "Max?"

He paused and sighed. "Yes, Emma?"

"Were you ever in love?"

He gripped the banister. "Once."

"What happened?"

"I went blind."

" 'S a rotten excuse." Her door closed softly.

"Yeah, it is," he whispered.

Three

"She broke into the house? For heaven's sake, Max. Did you have her arrested?"

"Of course not." Max rubbed his scar, wondering why he'd called his friend and associate in New York instead of waiting until Monday for his return. "I told you, Adam, she only wanted to present her campaign. Martha told me she didn't realize the poor woman was so desperate that she'd follow her to my house. I can't fault Emma for persistence."

"Poor woman? The last thing you need is another charity case!"

"I didn't mean that literally." He frowned. "At least, I don't think I do. I'm the boss, here, remember? I'm perfectly capable of judging the situation."

"That's not what I meant, and you know it. I've never known you to make a bad business decision. But you have to admit this whole thing stinks. And not with perfume."

"Something is wrong, that's for sure. She's almost frantic about selling us this scent, and I can't figure out why."

"Which means you can't leave it alone." It wasn't

a question. "Hiring a bunch of bums is one thing, Max. This is a big chunk of money."

"You were an outfielder not a bum."

"*Moi?* I was speaking of Martha and Benno, not *my* amazingly virile self."

Max heard the hint of sarcasm that always crept into Adam's voice when he spoke of himself. "And what is your amazingly virile opinion on the subject?"

"Depends on the lady's legs." His laughter died. "Maybe this perfume's stolen," he said gently. "Remember that problem last year?"

"She's not a felon." Absolute certainty rang in his voice.

Adam chuckled. "A strange woman breaks into your home, and you tell me she's not a felon?"

Max couldn't help but smile. Adam Daniels twisted his words around with the ease of long practice. "I'm convinced that her formula is her company's, and that it's real."

"So now what?"

"I'm going to buy it."

Adam groaned. "I've just finished the biggest campaign in our history, and you want another one? You're going to kill me, Max, and deprive all those sexy as yet unmet single ladies out there of the experience of a lifetime."

"Can it, Adam. You'll have to do very little with this one. She's got the whole damned thing mapped out!"

"You're kidding. It's that good?"

"It's kind of raw, but yes, it's good. The woman is amazing! Did I tell you she made the bottle out of clay? And wait until you smell this stuff! You'll imagine you died and went to heaven."

"I hope she's not standing next to you. She'll up the price."

"She's in bed. And I'm not—"

"She's where?" Adam's shock was clear. "You haven't had a woman there since Shan—"

"Not my bed!"

"Really? Why not?"

"She's asleep, Adam. She's been that way all day." And he'd been bored to tears for the first time in his life. "I haven't touched her." Much, he amended in his mind.

"All right, Max, if you say so. Now what? Do we buy an untested formula outright?"

Max knew Adam was trying to subtly guide his judgment, and for once he didn't resent it. It kept him on an even keel. "No. I have a different plan. . . ."

An hour later Max put the finishing touches on the aromatic *coq au vin*, and wiped his hands on a dishtowel. He brought down the crystal wineglasses he rarely used and took them to the table, placing them carefully. His hands ran over the settings, the vase filled with fresh-cut roses, the lighted candles, and he nodded. Everything was perfect.

Perfect for business, he told himself firmly. He'd gone to such trouble only to create a relaxed atmosphere in which to discuss her proposal. And, he thought, he'd set the table with all the trimmings only because he'd fallen out of practice over the years. He usually cooked only for himself or Adam. Dinner between them was always very informal.

Max checked the silverware placement, and swore when he realized it was the fourth time he had done so. He took a deep breath to quell the irritating flock of butterflies that had suddenly decided to jitterbug in his stomach and went to awaken Emma.

The doorbell rang as he hit the first stair and, frowning, he turned. "Who is it?" he called.

"It's Barry, Mr. Morgan."

Barry Lawton was a young policeman, one Max had encountered often on his evening walks around the quiet, well-patrolled neighborhood. He opened the door, a puzzled smile on his face. "Is something wrong?"

"That's what I was going to ask, sir. I saw your lights and wondered . . ."

"Everything's fine, Barry. I—I have a guest."

"Oh. I didn't see a car, so I thought . . . shoot, I thought maybe you had a burglar."

Max worked to keep a straight face. "Not anymore."

"You mean you chased someone off?" Barry asked eagerly.

"It was a joke," Max said, immediately regretting his impulsive words. "Sorry to disappoint you."

He sighed. "I remembered the trouble you had last year at the plant, and I—never mind. Have a good evening, sir."

Max's stomach tightened. "I will, Barry. Good night."

"Good night, sir."

After locking the door, Max paced upstairs and to his left. Good grief, he felt like a teenager on his first date. Why didn't that thought anger him now as much as it had last night?

He knocked on the door but received no answer. He entered, calling her name softly. Only the even sounds of her breathing told him she was still there and dead to the world.

He moved to the bedside, his fingers sliding over the cotton sheet, reaching out to shake her shoulder. His hand met something soft instead of the delicate bones he remembered.

Emma moaned in her sleep. The skin at his fingertips puckered. Hot blood ebbed and flowed to every inch of his body as he realized he'd touched her bare breast.

He gasped and jerked his hand back, cursing his rapid reaction. Pavlov's dog could have taken lessons from his body, he thought. Emma Machlen had to leave, the sooner the better.

His hands clenched, but he decided against waking her. She was much safer in sleep, out of his way.

Once downstairs, Max hesitated only a moment before blowing out the candles.

Emma awoke to the muffled sound of birds chirping and the ever-present drone of the air conditioner. She blinked several times to clear the fog from her eyes. Her body floated on a cushion of eiderdown. Where was she? Was this heaven? No, it couldn't be. Ol' St. Peter wouldn't let her mouth taste like old gym socks.

The soft sound of a latch clicking galvanized her mind. Her gaze snapped to the hazy shape entering her bedroom. "Max!" she said with a gasp, and sat bolt upright, grabbing her head as it swam with her sudden movement. The bright quilt pooled around her waist, and the cool air hit her bared breasts. Her eyes widened as she glanced down. How did she get naked?

"Good morning," Max said warily as he opened the door wide.

She sneaked the sheet over her breasts in a gesture of defense, its caress triggering a memory . . . of hands?

"Good morning," she managed to croak.

Instinctively drawing that veil of hers around her, easing into the white sheet, she scanned frantically for her clothes. The room looked like something out of *Gone With the Wind*, she thought: polished, heavy furniture, a four-poster, even an armoire. Except for the trail of garments running from her bed to the door across the cream carpet, it was perfect.

"How do you feel?" he asked.

"Fine. Except for the Kleenex on my teeth."

"That's a nauseatingly vivid image."

She stiffened. "What time is it?"

"Eight-thirty."

Her gaze shifted to him, and her breath caught. Max's golden hair was slicked back, he wore nothing but a tantalizing strip of black cloth one could laughingly call a bathing suit, and she smelled the faint odor of chlorine. His shoulders nearly spanned the doorway, and the reddish hair on his chest arrowed down a flat belly.

"Did you touch my—" She cut herself off with a fiery blush.

He shifted his feet, a sheepish grin on his lips. "I, uh, tried to wake you up earlier. I was aiming for your shoulder."

Emma's eyes narrowed. He'd known exactly what she was talking about. "Why do I get the idea that's a convenient excuse?"

"You talk in your sleep."

"And you're trying to put me on the defensive." It suddenly occurred to her that neither her veil nor the sheet was protecting her from Max, that the second effort was because the first hadn't worked. She defiantly dropped both, and she squelched an odd, wistful wish that he could see her.

He shrugged. "Are you hungry?"

Her stomach rumbled. "Yes."

"I'll be down after my shower." He turned away.

In all her mother's lectures on the proper behavior of a lady, she couldn't remember a single one for this situation, but good manners stirred. "Should I start coffee or something?"

"No!" He spun around. "Don't you dare set foot in that kitchen!"

Taken aback, Emma could only gape as he fought his outburst.

"Sorry. You're my guest, Emma. I like to cook." He closed her door behind him.

What was that all about, she wondered, but forced his actions away as she tried to remember the previous night. Letting her head sink to her palms, she worked to piece the fragments of memory together. She'd been to a crafts shop, she remembered. She'd made a collect call to her friend Cissy, who'd cackled outrageously at her antics. Then she'd eaten greasy french fries at an all-night diner while she'd worked on the mock-up. After a quick trip to the bathroom to change her clothes, she'd reentered the house through the door she'd left unlocked. She also remembered typing, the muffled printing, and then . . . a kiss? Or was that just wishful thinking?

She touched her lips automatically, achingly aware of the phantom caress. It had been so sweet, so comforting. It hadn't demanded one-sided love. It hadn't been a contest of wills, a battle for her identity. The kiss had given approval, acceptance for who she was, and had chased the ghost of Danny like a blazing torch chased darkness.

There had been a conversation, hadn't there? About Danny and something Max had said.

You disrupt my life, his voice echoed.

"This is crazy," she whispered. She felt as if she'd been on a bender, but she hadn't touched liquor since that one and only time after high school graduation. But if she really talked in her sleep, there was no telling what she'd told him. Dammit, she didn't want him to buy Chameleon out of pity!

Emma shifted uncomfortably as her body made known a neglected duty. She'd been afraid to use Max's bathroom when she wasn't even supposed to be there. With a groan she stumbled from the bed, snagged her clothes, and fumbled into them as she ran out her door. Something pressed into her thigh, and she fleetingly remembered the knife Cissy had given her for "protection" that Emma had promptly put into her suitcase and forgotten until she'd needed it to help carve the bottle.

She found the bathroom easily, hurried to finish, then slipped out and flew down the stairs as she heard another door open somewhere. Max, she thought, on his way to his shower.

If she worked quickly, she could present her proposal to Max in plenty of time before she had to catch her plane at noon—if he wasn't ready to throw his unwanted houseguest out the door.

She smelled fresh coffee as she ran through the library, and her stomach surprised her with a violent hunger pang. She slowed her pace, glancing around the rooms she'd seen only in shadow before. The breakfast nook was decorated with a modern blue and white sofa and chair, and a glass-topped table with chrome chairs. A bright yellow and orange, very updated kitchen was off in the far corner, delineated by a continuous counter running around it. A sliding glass door led outside to a huge flagstone patio, which was scattered with planters overflowing with lush summer flowers. Max's house was absolutely lovely.

At least she'd remembered her shoes this time, she thought as she slipped them on. Then she sank to a stool at the counter that linked the kitchen and breakfast nook. Water began to run. The shower.

Her stomach rumbled, and she gazed longingly at the loaf of bread and canteloupe beside the sink, her head whirling. Why was she so hungry?

As the shower continued to run, Max's warning took on the tones of a dare. Her spine stiffened. "Who does he think he is?" she asked a copper pot. "He can't order me around!"

But it's his house, a little voice whispered.

"But I'm so hungry," she shot back.

"He told me not to set foot in the kitchen," she said aloud. Her eyes narrowed, then a wide grin spread across her face. "So I won't!"

Reviving childhood instincts, Emma climbed up on the spotless counter and crawled on her hands and knees. She found baking soda in a cabinet above the sink and scrubbed her teeth clean with a wet finger, grimacing at the taste. After replacing that, she popped two pieces of bread into the toaster and stuffed another into her mouth. Inching farther, she reached the canteloupe but realized the knife rack was too far away. Undaunted, she pulled out Cissy's gift, an ivory-handled lockback with a wicked-looking blade. She sliced the melon neatly in half, rinsed the knife, clicked it shut, and replaced it in her pocket, resisting the urge to bury her mouth in the juicy orange flesh of the fruit.

"A spoon," she muttered, and glanced around. No spoon on the counter, but maybe he kept the silverware in the drawer beside the stove.

On her elbows and knees, the precious melon cradled in her hands, Emma crawled to the stove, then reached over and opened the drawer. "Ah-ha!" She grabbed a spoon and dug in. Juice dribbled from the corner of her mouth as she ate greedily. "Ambrosia," she mumbled, and dug out another hunk.

The toaster clicked behind her, signaling the near end of its cycle. She frowned, her mouth full. "Hmm, a small logistics problem." She could hardly grab it with her toes, so she inched backward again, her blue tank top bunching up underneath her breasts. When the cold metal of the sink touched her bared belly, she giggled. This was too easy!

Footsteps echoed in the hall with a sound like thunder, and Dixie entered, followed by a damp-haired Max clad in skintight jeans and a shirt. Emma froze, her eyes wide with apprehension.

"Ready for breakfast, girl?" he asked, ruffling Dixie's ears. "Emma, what about you?"

You disrupt my life.

No, she groaned mentally as Max headed for the kitchen. If he found her stretched out on the counter like some prime roast, he'd slice her into little pieces.

"Emma?" he called with a puzzled frown, then he shrugged. "Did she go outside into the garden, Dixie? Huh? Can you capture the wind?"

Though his voice sounded quite strange, Emma didn't have time to analyze his odd choice of words. She began to inch slowly backward, praying as she hadn't in years. Watching Max open a cabinet for Dixie's food, she breathed a small sigh of relief as the crackle of paper hid her retreat. She even spared a quick glance of appreciation as he bent over. His tight jeans did nothing to disguise a wonderfully firm backside and long, muscular legs. And the open-throated yellow polo shirt emphasized his broad shoulders and perfect tan.

Realizing she'd paused in breathless admiration, she scoffed at herself and began moving again. When she felt her feet dangle into empty air, she smiled. She would make it.

The toast popped.

Max froze, then turned toward her with a frown. "What in the heck was that?" he muttered.

He walked toward the toaster, his hand outstretched. Her heart raced, and she glanced under her arm at the betraying appliance with an indignant mental expletive. Then Max paused, puzzled.

"Emma?"

The jig was up. Accept the consequences.

"It's my toast, Mr. Morgan. I couldn't wait." She sighed and slid quickly to a stool. His head followed her noisy movement, his amber eyes lit with an emotion she couldn't place.

"I see."

To her amazement, his lips twitched. But he turned quickly away and began to feed Dixie. She braced herself, waiting for the ax to fall.

"You didn't set foot in my kitchen," he said, trying to disguise the humor in his voice.

"No, Mr. Morgan. I didn't."

"Don't you think we're on a first-name basis by now?" he asked.

"Are we?"

He poured kibble into Dixie's bowl. "I think so. Hurricane Emma."

She shrugged, fighting remorse. She *had* acted like a hurricane, but he made her feel like a naughty schoolgirl. Just like old Mr. Wyler.

"Would you like to discuss my proposal now? I—I have to go soon." She sighed. "I have a plane to catch."

He poured her a cup of coffee, buttered her toast, and handed it all to her. "You do?"

Emma would have liked to think that disappointment shadowed his voice. "I do," she said softly, surprised at her own desire to stay. "That's why I worked all night."

Max frowned, turned to the refrigerator, and pulled out eggs, then groped on the counter, pausing for a moment before setting them down. "Emma? What day is it?"

"Saturday, of course."

He shook his head. "It's Sunday."

The room spun before her eyes. Disoriented, Emma could only think that she didn't have enough money to buy another ticket. And the cheap rental car was sitting around the corner, racking up time.

Her hands trembled. What would she tell everyone? Her parents wouldn't worry, since Cissy was covering for her, but her old friend would be frantic. She'd slept more than twenty-four hours! "No wonder I was so hungry," she whispered.

He turned away but didn't quite hide a fleeting smile. "I hope you like scrambled eggs. I don't do them any other way." He grabbed a small bowl from a high cupboard. "Oh, and Emma? Save some canteloupe for me."

Emma groaned and let her head thump to the counter.

"You'll need your strength over the next few days," he said gently.

Her head shot up. "Why?"

"Because I want you to duplicate the formula in a controlled environment." He paused. "Before I buy it."

"You—you're going to buy it?" Emma fought back a shout of joy. She'd done it! Everything was going to be all right! "Oh, Max, thank you!"

"Don't thank me," he said as he broke the eggs into the bowl and beat them savagely. "I'm not going to pay your price."

Dismay flooded her. "I can't go any lower, Max."

"I'm not asking you to. I want to buy it on a percentage-of-sales basis. You'll make ten times the amount you're asking in the first year if it does as well as I think it will."

"But—" She couldn't tell him she needed the money almost immediately. Her pride wouldn't let her. If it was good enough for Daniels Cosmetics, someone else would snap it up. "Then I'm afraid I can't sell it to you."

"Emma," he said with a sigh. "No one is going to risk money on an untested product."

"It's been tested! My sister Diana is a pharmacognostic researcher. I have the documentation for allergic reactions, chemical breakdown, the works! She—"

"I mean market tested."

"Oh." Her mind worked quickly. Whether he was right about the other companies or not, the fact was that she didn't have enough money or time to try again. "How long before we realize a profit?"

"It depends. Market testing shouldn't take long, and we could be in full production by the time we get the results back."

Emma realized what a gamble he was willing to take with that statement. He was trusting his instincts; surely she could trust hers—and him. "Can we begin immediately?"

"Of course. We'll start first thing tomorrow morning."

Why did things have to be so complicated, she wondered wistfully. She glanced up, watching Max for several moments as he poured the eggs into the pan and stirred them. The muscles in his back rippled with his slightest movement, and she found herself staring with a hunger that had nothing to do with food. His hair had dried touseled, the morning lighting the golden strands with fire.

Her pulse quickened. There was beauty in his soul, she knew instinctively, though he was good at hiding it. She was an expert on concealment, but she didn't want to hide from him. She felt connected to him in a way she'd never been before.

She wanted to stay, to explore these new feelings. "Max, I—"

"What are your plans for the day?" he asked quickly, as if sensing the sudden change in the atmosphere. He stood rigid, and she knew he had no intention of inviting her to spend it with him. Irrationally it hurt. Did he shut everyone out? Or just her?

You disrupt my life.

She swallowed a tightness in her throat. "Sightseeing," she said with a forced cheerfulness. "I have a lot of ground to cover."

"Good." He dished up the fluffy eggs and set them before her, nearly slamming the plate to the counter. "Eat fast or they'll get cold."

Emma's ire rose. What he meant was "Eat fast and get the hell out of my life."

Her gray eyes narrowed. How could she ever have thought there was any softness in him? How had she ever supposed there was something between them, something magical? She wouldn't stay if he begged her to! If she had to sleep in that filthy wreck of a car, and she probably would, she'd be damned if she ever showed him how vulnerable she really was to him. "I just lost my appetite." She stood and turned quickly. "See you tomorrow, Max."

She ran from the house as if all the demons of hell were chasing her.

Max spent half the morning cursing his outburst and the other half telling himself it was for the best. He wondered why she was so desperate, then told himself it wasn't important. He began to erase any trace of Emma Machlen from his house by stripping the sheets from the bed in which she'd slept.

Her scent lingered on the soft cotton, and his mind gave him a vivid image of her breasts under his fingertips. His body tightened. "Damn!" he whispered.

Why couldn't he forget her? Why had it hurt so much to chase her out this morning? Why didn't he just give in to his urges and get her out of his system once and for all? Passion didn't last, and that was something he knew he could control.

He shook himself, cursing his weakness. How could he even consider a sexual relationship with her? She'd been nothing but trouble from the first moment. In a few days she'd be out of his life, and that's exactly what he wanted.

As he dusted the room, he found her bra draped drunkenly over a chair in the corner. "It's not my day," he told Dixie.

Sometime after lunch the phone rang. Max answered it, and his pulse quickened at the voice at the other end. It was Emma. "How did you get my number?" he demanded.

"It was sort of in plain sight."

"Sort of where?"

"Uh, on a note in the library." He heard dishes

rattling in the background. "Under a big stack of papers."

His mouth twitched. "And naturally you had to try it out."

"Naturally. Okay, I'll admit, there's another reason."

"You wanted to remind me to lock my door."

"That too." She laughed, but it had a hard edge to it. "I don't suppose I left something there, did I?"

"You mean besides your bra?"

"Oh, Lord, I didn't even realize *that* was gone. No, I mean my . . . my wallet?"

He remembered placing it on his desk the morning he'd awakened her at the computer. The morning he'd kissed her. "Yes, it's here." Something twisted inside him when he realized there was panic in her voice. "What's wrong?"

"Nothing's wrong," she said quickly, but he heard an angry male voice behind hers, demanding money.

"Emma, where are you?"

She hesitated. "In a restaurant near Forest Park."

He sighed. Even when she was gone, he couldn't get rid of her. "I'll have Benno run it over."

"Thanks." She struggled with herself for a moment. "I won't trouble you again, Max."

"No trouble, Emma."

He bundled the bra and wallet into a paper bag so as not to offend Benno's sensibilities, and sent them off. Afterward he turned on the stereo and let the soothing strains of a Brahms symphony wash over him. By dinnertime his house was almost back to normal, peaceful and his alone. It was only that night, in his empty bed, that memories plagued him. Finally, though, he fell into a restless sleep.

When the phone rang again, he awakened with a jerk and snatched it from its cradle, knocking the rest of the telephone off the nightstand with a resounding crash. "What?" he nearly shouted into the receiver.

The line crackled for a moment, then he heard her voice again. "Max?"

Of course, he thought. Who else would it be? He sunk his head into his hand and yawned, then reached out for his clock and felt the braille numbers. "Good Lord! It's after three!"

"Shoot, I was hoping you didn't have a clock."

Max frowned. It wasn't simple panic he heard in her voice this time. "I swear I don't have your wallet."

"I know. The desk sergeant took it and doesn't seem to want to give it back. Can you imagine?"

Something clanged in the background, echoes of other voices drifted to him. Cold fear twisted in the pit of his stomach. Under her brave laughter Emma Machlen was scared to death. "What's wrong?"

"A funny thing happened on the way to the plant."

Had she been mugged? Or worse? Fury built, fast and heavy, heating his blood. "Are you hurt, Emma?" he asked in a low, dangerous tone. If anyone had touched her . . .

"Not exactly. I—" She swallowed audibly. "I'm in jail, Max. I need you to come bail me out!"

Four

"Hi, Max! I guess I really did it this time, huh?"

At the sound of Emma's falsely repentant voice, Max wondered whether he should strangle her first, or grab her and hold her tight, or burst into laughter. In the hours he'd spent waiting, he'd contemplated all three.

In the end he retained his rationality and did none of them. Now that he knew she was safe, though, like a parent who's just saved his child from walking in front of a speeding car, Max wanted to shake her.

Clutching the bail slip tightly in his hand, Max shifted in the uncomfortable metal chair. "You are the most aggravating woman." He shook his head ruefully. "Only Emma Machlen could fall asleep in a car that was used for a series of burglaries."

She sat beside him and laughed unsteadily. "It's my criminal tendencies, Max. They finally won out over my . . ." She trailed off and cleared her throat.

That brave quiver almost undid him, but he resisted the urge to wrap her in his arms. Unless he wanted to walk facefirst into a wall, he'd need to concentrate on his surroundings. Ringing phones, voices raised in argument, the tinny voice of the dispatcher, all echoed acutely in his mind. He couldn't give in to the irrational feeling that they would trample him. He had to filter them out.

"How do you get yourself into these things?" he asked with a smile.

"It's a talent," she said. "Your lawyer is nice, Max. Thanks for calling him."

Max tensed. Emma was much too subdued. "What did he say about this whole thing?"

"He said—" Her voice lowered to a baritone. " 'Ms. Machlen, I hope you appreciate the seriousness of the charges against you.' "

Max grinned at her perfect imitation of his lawyer Jim's stuffy voice. "After which, you, of course, giggled in his face."

"Of course! It's all a mistake. The burglaries were committed by a ring of out-of-state thieves who flew into town, robbed houses, then flew out without a trace. It was the same kind of setup that foiled the police at your plant."

Of course it was a mistake. Max knew that with certainty, though why he was so sure baffled him. "Ah! That's why you're so good at breaking into houses!" he said in mock realization.

"Naturally." Her preening tone didn't quite cover her apprehension. "Thanks for telling them those designs weren't yours, Max. It saved me from the grand theft charge."

He swallowed heavily and stood. "Are you ready to go?"

"Sure. I guess I'll meet you at the plant later, huh?"

"No, Emma," he said sternly. "I'm not taking any chances. I can't let you loose on an unsuspecting public. Benno's waiting outside. I'm taking you home with me."

"You don't have to do that! I won't—"

"No arguments, Emma. This"—he waved the

bail bond in the air—"makes me responsible for you." He grasped the handle of Dixie's harness. "Your arraignment is tomorrow morning, and I'm going with you."

She hesitated. "Max? I keep you busier than a one-armed paperhanger, don't I?"

Max turned away and smiled. "Yes, you do."

"I wouldn't have called you if I'd known anyone else in town."

"I know that."

She hesitated again. "Max, though I appreciate your lawyer, he's corporate. I seem to need the criminal type. A public defender."

"Is it the money?"

"We're going to go 'round like a button on a barn door about this, aren't we?" She sighed. "Of course it's the money. They impounded my car, which was rented, and they told me you're paying the fees. I'll pay you back."

"Don't worry about it," he said tersely, and walked toward the door.

Emma stared after him for a moment, sighed, then picked up her suitcase and drawings and followed him. She shouldn't have called him, she thought disgustedly. In the hours following her arrest she'd deeply regretted her impulse. But she felt so safe with him. The moment she'd seen him she'd wanted to run and throw her arms around him. Only the knowledge that he didn't want her in his life had stopped her. One sign, one little gesture from him, and she would have thrown herself at him.

He disturbed her more than she would ever admit. After twenty-seven years of butting heads with overdeveloped egos, of hiding behind her illusions, she had proven that she could hold her own in any battle of wills. But Max confused her. One minute he was ready to laugh with her, which she'd learned a long time earlier was her best defense, yet the next he acted as if he couldn't care less. His tense posture told her he was angry. She hadn't seen anyone that mad since she'd put Ben-Gay in her sister Diana's bra after she'd unfairly compared their bust sizes.

Damnation, she shouldn't have called him! If it hadn't been for that dark cell . . .

When she stepped into the bright morning sunlight, she flinched and hissed as it stung her eyes.

"What's wrong?" Max asked, turning in instant concern.

"Nothing. Just tasting freedom, I guess." She drew a deep breath of air. For the first time in hours she smiled with true happiness. "Lord, I hate being cooped up."

"Did they—they didn't hurt you or anything, did they?"

Her brows raised, she peered into Max's face. His anger had disappeared, and she saw the smudges under his tawny eyes, the lines of fatigue that had formed around his mouth. "Max, I grew up on a postage stamp of an island, the only goldfish in a tankful of Siamese fighting fish. I'm used to having a bunch of people around me."

"Emma—"

"Things happen, Max. Just because I went through *Hill Street Blues* via *The Twilight Zone*, you think I'm not okay? I'm as tough as an old nut!"

He stepped closer, reaching for her arm, and held it in a firm grip. "Don't joke about this, Emma. Did anyone hurt you?" he repeated, his words intense.

Emma's heart constricted. Maybe he cared a little, she thought, and tenderly touched a crease on his brow, smoothing the line with her fingertip. "It's been a long time since anybody's worried about me," she whispered in wonder. "I think I like it."

She leaned forward and did what she'd longed to do since she'd met him. She kissed him.

Max felt the brush of her lips on his, a touch, a simple thank-you, but his hands clenched on her arms with the depth of his reaction. His entire body shivered with the sensation her warm mouth caused. He wanted to crush her to him and explore the moist recesses, to taste the woman who'd haunted his existence. He wanted to throw her down right there and strip her naked, touching her silky skin in a way he'd only dreamed of.

But he'd be damned if he'd let her do this to him again. By sheer force of will he fought the emotions that welled to the surface, and set her firmly aside. "I wasn't worried," he said. "I was concerned, that's all. I just want to keep you out of trouble."

Emma watched him turn away, puzzled. She'd felt his hands on her arms and had thought for a moment that he would draw her to him. But he hadn't. He'd fought her instead, and that hurt her more than she'd ever dreamed possible. Just when she thought he might be different, that he might show some true tenderness, he'd shut down. He wanted everything on his terms. Fine, just fine. Maxwell Morgan was made of stone, and she was too tired to go excavating again.

Damnation, he was as hard and unyielding as Danny. And if she let him, Max would steamroll her too. "You've got more brass than an army mule," she said in disbelief. "You dare to presume you or anyone else is my keeper?"

"I don't see anyone lining up for the job!" Max had left himself wide open with that remark, and he knew it. He almost hoped she'd take the chance he offered. It would make things so much easier.

She didn't. "I'm twenty-seven years old," she said stiffly. "I'm perfectly capable of taking care of myself. I've been doing it for a long, long time."

"You're so good at it that you didn't have sense enough to ask for a place to sleep."

"I had a place to sleep."

"Your car!"

"I've done it before."

He bit his lip. "Just what in the hell were you doing sleeping in your car anyway?"

"No room at the inn?" she quipped faintly.

"Dammit, don't start with me! I know you need money. Tell me why!"

She turned away, resenting his arrogant tone. "It's not your problem, Max."

Max opened his mouth but then closed it tightly.

They fell into an uneasy silence until Benno arrived with the car, and the silence held until they were on the highway. Max turned his face away from her, afraid his expression might reveal just how frightened he'd been. He couldn't afford to show her how close he was to laughter either. In spite of her ordeal, Emma Machlen continued to come up with the most outrageous images. Dammit, he *wanted* to be angry with her! He wanted to resent her intrusion! She'd done nothing but turn his life upside down since she'd blown into it. He wished the image he had of her body in his arms were less vivid.

"The barometer grass should arrive tomorrow," said Emma. "I called, and they're expressing it out."

"Good. The sooner you get started . . ."

The sooner she'd be gone. He didn't say the words, but he meant them, and Emma knew it.

Benno dropped her at the house, and Emma couldn't wait to escape the car. Max didn't say a word as Benno unlocked the door and let her in, but couldn't resist a parting shot.

"Put those designs somewhere safe," he called. "We don't want anyone else stealing them!"

She bit back a nasty remark.

After they left, she took her drawings into the

library and set them carefully on Max's desk. They were his now, after all. Then she took her suitcase up to the room that she'd slept in before, assuming that's where she'd be staying.

As she opened her valise, she gasped. Everything had been tossed into it haphazardly, unlike her neat packing job. "Oh, Lord," she whispered. "They went through my clothes too!"

The horrors of the last hours repeated themselves vividly in her mind, her claustrophobic fear of the tiny jail cell, the suspicious-looking women who'd occupied it. Only her veil had protected her from their attentions, and she'd been absolutely terrified.

With a moan she bundled everything back into the suitcase and ran downstairs into the basement, hoping there was a washing machine there. An iron band seemed to tighten around her chest as she searched frantically. It had suddenly become imperative that she feel clean.

She found the washer beneath the wooden stairs, and she jerked open the lid, threw all her clothes into it, and tossed in a cupful of soap. Her own filthy state didn't escape her notice, and she peeled off her jeans and T-shirt, then her bra and panties, and shoved them in too. She slammed the lid and punched the cycle button, furious to find that her hands were shaking.

She felt her skin crawl, whether in memory or some other reason, and she raced back upstairs to the bathroom. She turned the shower as hot as she could stand it, and scrubbed every square inch of her body until it burned. She washed her hair three times.

Tears blended with the water, but Emma clenched her teeth and swallowed the knot in her chest. "Damnation," she said. "Don't do this!"

There was only one person who could help her regain her perspective. Wrapping a towel firmly around her, she ran downstairs and placed a collect call. It went through quickly, and Cissy's familiar raspy voice answered. "What's wrong?" was her first question, and Emma rolled her gray eyes to heaven.

"Is it just me," she asked, "or do you scare everybody with that line?"

"When a Machlen calls," Cissy said with a chuckle, "it's inevitable that there's trouble." Her laughter quickly turned into a cough.

"Quit smoking," said Emma automatically.

"Quit stalling," Cissy shot back. "You called me last night, Emma-love. Everything was milk and honey then in spite of the bumpy start with your Apollo, so I assume somethin's happened to throw a fox in the chicken coop."

"Nothing I can't handle." She fought her tears.

"I don't like the sound'a that, sweetie."

"When are you leaving for London, you nosy old biddie?"

"Thursday. I'll be in St. Louis in a couple of weeks for some charity do, but you'll be gone by then."

"I'm not sure about that," said Emma. "I might be here longer than I'd expected."

"It's not a hitch in your perfume, is it? You're already cuttin' it as close as a wasp's whisker with this marketing thing and—"

"No, Cissy, it's got nothing to do with that. How does Uncle Jason like running the company?"

Cissy groaned. "He's havin' the time of his life. Just don't get him talkin' about it. He'll bend your ear right off!"

Emma hesitated. "Have there been any more problems?"

"Whoever it is who's been hasslin' ya'll, honey, is biding his sweet time. They think they got you, and they're just playin' jackal, waitin' for the lions to leave the pickin's."

"As long as nobody says anything to anyone."

"The Machlen clan sticks together like barnacles on a ship when they're threatened, you know that. Your momma and daddy were worried sick when I told them what you'd done. Raised hell for a solid hour with me for lettin' you too. Your aunt threatened me with shingles if I ever helped you again."

Emma grimaced. She knew what it was like to be at the receiving end of one of her family's famous tongue-lashings. And Aunt Rose's dire threats usually worked. But Cissy always gave as good as she got. "They'll get over it. They always do. Machlens don't hold grudges."

"So," she said, "if it's not the perfume, what's keepin' you there? All right, honey. Spill it."

Emma did. She told her the entire story of her arrest, leaving out Max's behavior and her own apprehensions. Cissy would know that anyway, and it was best forgotten. "So you see," she finished with a chuckle, "it was all a mistake. The car's plate number hadn't cleared their computer."

"You called Max when you could'a called me to wire you the bail money?" Cissy questioned.

Emma warmed all over at the mention of his name, but shook it off. "He was closer. It's really kind of funny, Cissy. Max wants me out so bad he can taste it, but he's stuck with me. He paid my bail. He signed for me. Does that mean he owns me? You know, I thought slavery was ab—"

Cissy sighed. "Look, Emma-love. I know it's none of my business—"

"That never stopped you before," she said with a feeble attempt at humor.

"—but for years I've watched you run like a jackrabbit with its tail on fire every time you get close to someone. I know you're attracted to Max by what you're *not* saying, and that Max is a strong man."

"Like a wall."

"Honey, just because a man is strong doesn't mean he'll take your soul. Danny was a selfish man, and you were a lot younger then. You fell in love and gave him everything, it's your nature. You jump in with both feet and usually sink up to your neck. But you're a hell of a lot more stubborn than you were when you lived with him. You come out on top these days. Besides, some men give as well as take."

"Do they?"

"Yes, they do. Now," she said cheerfully, sounding more like the Cissy of old. "I want to tell you about Evan's latest stunt."

Emma listened to Cissy's tale of her agent, of a chorus girl, and something about a chicken, but her mind wasn't really on it. She thought of Cissy's advice, implied if not given. She was right. If there was any tenderness in Max, if he stopped fighting human emotions, she knew what would happen—she'd fall like a ton of bricks.

Well, she thought. No fear of that.

"I have to go, Cissy. Good-bye."

She sighed. "Good-bye, Emma-love. Take care of yourself."

"I always do."

Emma hung up and stared into the shadows of the library for long moments. Then she shook herself. She needed movement, activity. She went downstairs. After tossing her clothes into the dryer, except for the one thing she could stand wearing wet—her bathing suit—she explored the basement, finding all the equipment she'd need for the next day, when the barometer grass arrived. She tested the tiny hotplate and found the ceramic dishes. Deciding to experiment, she pulled down a small bunch of fragrant sage from among the dried herbs hanging from the ceiling and began to work.

Hours later, lost in her occupation, she almost missed the sound. Someone was moving around upstairs. Max would have called out to her, wouldn't he have? The blood rushed from her face, and she tiptoed to the bottom of the basement stairs, listening intently.

Footsteps sounded, coming her way. With a frantic glance around she darted behind the freestanding counter, letting herself flow into it, veiling herself. Just in case, she thought.

A man came into view. A tall, lanky, *dark*-haired man who definitely wasn't Max. Frozen with apprehension, she watched as he checked her suitcase, swept the room with his gaze, then went back upstairs. Emma sat, numb. What could she do? Who was he?

Then she heard an unfamiliar male voice murmuring something, and she went cold all over.

"Oh, no," she whispered, Max's warning ringing in her ears. "It's a real thief!"

Five

"What do you mean, she's not there?"

Adam pulled the receiver away from his ear at Max's roar, his blue eyes widening at the string of expletives that followed. When the yelling died down, he settled the phone back. "I only said I couldn't find her, Max. Her suitcase is on top of the washer, her clothes are in the dryer—she's got to be around here somewhere. Listen carefully, *I'll find her.* I only called you because you said you'd sit on the phone until I did." Adam chuckled. "Good grief, it hasn't been that long since you dropped her off. What kind of trouble can she get into in a couple of hours?"

Max's silence was tense. "I'll be there in five minutes," he said.

"No, don't—"

The line went dead, and Adam stared at the receiver for several moments before hanging up. Then he picked up the designs from Max's desk and carefully looked over them.

In the kitchen Emma slipped silently to the counter, reaching for the telephone with shaking hands. Then she stopped. The police wouldn't believe her. They'd think she'd stolen the designs and covered it with a wild story. Lord, what could she do?

Calm down, she told herself firmly, wasting precious minutes. She needed to think. Think.

Her roving gaze fell on the tall, narrow closet beside the stove. Her pulse leapt as she stole toward it. With any luck Max kept his cleaning supplies there. She opened it, grimacing at the whisper of sound it made. Inside she found the broom, mop, and vacuum cleaner. Emma reached for her choice of weapon and turned toward the library.

She'd be damned if she'd let this thief escape unscathed, she thought as she crept up to her unsuspecting victim.

Some instinct, born of years of ducking wild pitches, made Adam turn. Just in time to see a whirlwind in a turquoise bikini clobber him.

Emma drew the broom back and prepared for another strike. "Get out of here!" she shouted.

The tall, ebon-haired man gaped, but recovered quickly. "You're going to hurt someone with that!" he cried, and reached for the broom.

Emma stepped back and walloped him again. "That's the idea, buster. You're not going to steal those designs if I have anything to say about it!" She swung, but he ducked and grabbed the handle.

"Hey, I'm not the one sneaking around here. I'm—"

Emma jerked the broom out of his hands and swung again. "This isn't your house!"

Adam retreated behind Max's big leather chair. "You're quite a little spitfire, aren't you?" he asked as he stared at her.

Taking advantage of his brief distraction, she darted around, but Adam kept the chair between them. He dodged, she intercepted, and he took off through the opening, running into the parlor.

She was close on his heels. Adam picked up a spindly side chair and held it in front of him like a lion tamer while she swung again. He was having trouble holding back his laughter. "You *must* be Emma Machlen!"

She froze, her eyes narrowing. "And who must you be?"

"Adam Daniels. Max's executive everything. I'm supposed to look over your designs!"

"Hold it!" She raised her broom again. "You're in New York!"

"I am?" Adam pretended surprise. "You mean this is all a dream, and I'll wake up in my stuffy hotel room?" He dropped the chair and placed his hand over his heart. "Thank heavens. Something like this could scar my ego for life. Imagine the stories in the locker room!" He spread his hands before him as if envisioning a headline. "Adam Daniels, macho ex-baseball player, beaten by Little Bit."

Her weapon dipped slightly as she weighed the truth of his words, a reluctant grin pulling at her mouth. Before she had time to swing again, he pounced. One hand snagged the broom and tossed it aside, the other spun her around. In no time at all he had her squirming, slender body slung over his shoulder. "You're something, do you know that? With my brains and your brawn, we could be quite a team."

"Put me down!" she shrieked. The man was insane! He was holding her prisoner and propositioning her! "Let me loose this minute, or I swear I'll show you how many dirty tricks I know."

"Oh, baby, if you're worried about Max—"

She tossed her head, no easy task while upside down. "I'm not worried about Max—"

"I wish someone were worried about me," came a dry voice from the doorway.

Emma groaned. Death was too good for Adam Daniels.

"Adam, is there a problem?"

"Your little felon had me pinned in the corner

with a broom, Max. I really think you should have warned her that I was back."

Blood rushed to Emma's face. Mortified, she peeked under Adam's arm, hoping it was a clever imitation. No such luck. It was Max. "Your friend was rifling your desk. What else was I supposed to think?"

Adam swatted her fanny playfully, and she yelped. Max's face darkened in fury, and he actually took a step forward before reining in his anger. "Did he hurt you?" Max asked.

"Don't you mean 'she'?" cried Adam, a single brow raised at Max's behavior and Emma's sudden tension. "This lady swings a mean broom!"

"Subtle as a freight train, Mr. Daniels."

"Mister?" He held his hand to his heart. "I'm offended. I'm hurt. I'm—"

"Overacting," Emma said blandly. "Put me down."

Adam grinned. "Please, I'm emoting here. And call me Adam. In view of the, er, view, I think you've earned it." He cleared his throat and began again. "Lady, for you I'd climb the highest mountain, swim the widest sea—"

"Plow the deepest furrow." Her voice echoed his tone exactly. "Oh, weren't you finished?" she asked contritely. "I'm sorry, it's all this blood rushing to my brain. I just wanted to see how deep it would go before I had to get out my hip boots."

"Max, help. She's vicious!"

Max listened to their exchange, amazed by the most irrational stab of jealousy. Why should he care what they were doing? Why should it bother him that Emma was obviously enjoying Adam's company far more than she did his? It was nothing to him! Max bared his teeth in a semblance of a smile. "Sorry, Adam. I've never heard you so neatly shot down before. It's quite an education." He turned away. "Since I know my house is safe, Emma, I'll return to the plant. Adam, since you two seem to be getting along so well, why don't you take her to lunch? I'm sure she's starved. Unless she's been on the counters again."

"No, my crawling days are over."

Max heard a double entendre in her remark but refused to let it bother him.

"Lunch," said Adam, "sounds great. Emma, run upstairs and put some clothes on. I'll wait."

Put some clothes on?

The words echoed in his brain. "Adam, you have one hour. You have a lot of work to catch up on." Max spun on his heel.

"By the way, Max. You were right to trust her. She has great legs. And a little mole just over her left—"

Damning Adam, Emma, and most of all himself, Max stormed from the house, cutting off Adam's words. The woman was the plague, and he would be a fool to catch it.

Over the next few days tension tightened in Max's house. The barometer grass arrived Tuesday morning, and Emma began the process of extracting its essence. Max had put the entire project under tight security—employees worked on different pieces but not the whole—and Emma would use his stillroom in the basement of the house to create the key ingredient, the fixative, the component that would pull each of the sixteen separate scents together into the unique fragrance that was Chameleon.

Despite his resolve to avoid her, Max was interested in her process and stayed with her while she worked with the grass. She first soaked the tough, reedlike strands in a baking soda bath, explaining that it would dissolve the hard, acidic outer layer. The grass actually changed color in its natural habitat, she told him, from yellow to green to brown, depending on the amount of moisture and pressure in the air, which was why it had been named barometer grass. After allowing four hours for it to soak in the soda water, she pounded it with a mortar and pestle and placed it carefully in a small vat of simmering almond oil for twenty minutes, then set it aside. There it would stay until Friday, with only an occasional stirring to hasten the rendering process.

Their hands brushed just once. Emma's hair touched Max's cheek, bringing with it the scent that haunted him. And Max flew from the house to bury himself in work.

On Wednesday Adam still hadn't begun to clear away the mountain of work that Max had set before him, and he'd had no time for Emma or Max for that reason. But Adam grinned at the tactic. He watched in silent amusement as Max double-booked a shipment of crystal bottles, listened to his computerized inventory four times before he'd heard any of it, and ran Martha ragged with contradictory orders all afternoon. When Adam chuckled, Max barked, "And why haven't you been haunting the house as usual?"

"I had the oddest feeling you didn't want me there."

Max sighed and rubbed his neck. "I'm sorry, Adam. It's not you. It's . . . *her*." He shook his head. "I came home yesterday and found her at the top of the built-in bookcase, stuck. She'd climbed up there without a chair and couldn't get down! She—"

Max gulped. He'd reached up to help her down, and she'd trustingly fallen into his arms like a ripe peach. She'd touched his scar and had gently asked him how he'd gotten it.

"I had a disagreement with a tree," he'd told her. "I lost."

And then he'd put her firmly on her feet, turning away before his obvious arousal betrayed him. Cold showers had no effect, even his rowing machine was beginning to show signs of strain. Though Adam had somehow become the intruder, Max needed the buffer.

"Please come to dinner," Max said finally. "I'd like the company."

"I wouldn't miss it for the world," Adam said softly.

That evening Max stormed into the house and bellowed for Emma. She descended the stairs, book in hand, dressed in jeans and a pink tank top. She threw a speaking glance Adam's way, then they both followed Max into the kitchen.

"Don't let that lion growl bother you," Adam whispered as they went. "I love that man like a brother, but sometimes he can be rather intimidating."

"I'm not intimidated," she shot back quickly, her eyes flashing. "I'm terrified."

He chuckled and gallantly held out a stool at the counter. Once settled, her gaze never left Max's back as he moved easily around his familiar kitchen, preparing what appeared to be a chef's salad. As Max ravaged the lettuce, Emma asked what she could do to help.

"Nothing," said Max stiffly. "I'm perfectly capable of fixing dinner myself. I'm not an invalid."

"I never said you were," she said softly. "I'm not used to sitting around all day doing nothing, that's all."

Max's hands stilled for a moment, then went on to stab tomatoes. "Is that because of your family?" he asked with seeming casualness. "Do you work yourself so hard for the money?"

Her mouth firmed. "I do my part. Max, isn't there something that I can do around here? Typing, anything?"

Max decimated a radish. "You can't afford any

more trouble. Just sit there like a good little girl and do exactly what you're told to do, all right?"

Her eyes narrowed, then a wicked smile crept across her face. "All right, Max," she said demurely. "I will."

Though Max frowned suspiciously, he said nothing. After finishing the salad, he ferried plates, wine, and glasses to the glass-topped table, then served each of them a monster portion. Adam moved to a chair and raised his brows when Emma made no move to join them. She mimicked his gesture and remained at the counter.

When Max realized she hadn't seated herself, he turned to her. "Come and sit down, Emma. I promise I haven't laced the salad with arsenic."

"Yes, Max," she said, and flowed from her stool to the table. Then she sat. On the floor.

Adam's eyes widened. What was she up to?

"So, Emma," Max said with an attempt at polite conversation as he sat in his chair, "what did you do today?"

As she began to outline in excruciating detail the events of her day, Max frowned, and his head turned in her direction. "Emma," he said, cutting her off. "Where are you?"

"On the floor."

His mouth worked. "Would you care to join us at the table?"

"I would like that."

He waited, but she didn't move. "Emma," he said through clenched teeth. "Sit in a chair, please."

She did, smiling.

Adam's gaze darted between them. "So, uh, Emma. I meant to ask you. Who is that stunning woman in your designs?"

"My sister," she said shortly.

"Does she have a name?"

"Diana."

"Do you have any more at home like her?"

A pregnant pause followed his words. "Emma doesn't like to talk about her family, Adam," said Max smugly. "Find another subject."

Emma's chin tilted up. "I have two sisters, Adam. And three brothers." With a grin at Max's frustrated expression she continued. "And two parents, my mother's sister and my father's brother are there, too, married to each other. They're British, but my father's family had owned Machlen Island for generations. They had one side of the house, we had the other. Then, of course, there are my seven cousins, various spouses, and their children—"

"All on the same island?" asked Max, astonished.

Her face softened just for an instant. "Most of the time. And you, Max?"

Max's expression shuttered. "I was an only child."

"Oh," she whispered, and her hand crept toward his, then stopped.

After a tense moment of silence Max barked, "I think we need some music. Turn on the stereo, Emma."

She stiffened and flew from the room.

"Max," Adam said softly, "I think you're being a little rough on her."

"I know," Max said, rubbing his scar. "But she makes me feel like an extra in *Alice in Wonderland*. I don't know what to do with her!"

Emma slipped back to the table, and Max sat straight. "I can't hear the stereo."

Emma cocked her head. "Neither can I."

"Well, turn it up."

"Yes, Max." With a giggle that belied her words of obedience, she raced out again. Quite a bit later she returned and sat once again.

"I still can't hear the stereo," Max said patiently.

"No, Max," she said, and took a bite of her salad.

"Did you turn it up?"

"Of course. I did *exactly* what you told me to do."

Max stood. "I'll do it."

She just smiled.

Adam looked at her curiously after Max had left, then his eyes opened wide in surprise as a strangled chuckle came from the library. "I release you from your vow, Emma!" Max called.

Adam turned to Emma. "What did you do?" he whispered.

"Turned up the stereo." She shrugged. "Well, only the tuner. The rest of it was too heavy."

Adam laughed and shook his head. "I think I've been waiting for you all my life," he said. "Max is in deep trouble."

She smiled an oddly wistful smile and picked at her salad.

Emma spent the next day restlessly prowling Max's house. She swam in his pool, explored his vibrant rose garden, but nothing seemed to calm her. Anxiety for her family's deadline, horrible fears that she'd totally screw up the test batch, and, worst of all, Max's hostility all made her feel like a turkey being force fed for the slaughter. She spread a towel on the flagstone patio beside the pool and told herself to sleep. The relentless sun beat down on her and did nothing to aid her.

Finally, with a groan, she jumped up and ran into the house, grabbed her shampoo and body oil, and headed to the bathroom.

After nearly an hour the hot shower melted the knots of tension in her muscles. Everything would work out, she told herself. It always did. She twisted a towel over her hair and fixed another around her wet body. With a smile she opened the oil, a different version of the Chameleon fragrance, and smoothed it over her damp skin, taking her time with her long legs.

Serene, she capped the bottle, gathered her clothes, and juggled everything into her arms. The knot at her breast began to give, and she hugged herself. It was a short trip after all.

With another look around the bathroom to assure herself she'd left it tidy, she opened the door and let loose a cloud of scented steam. The knot unwound, but her arms kept the towel at her breast as she began to pace toward her room.

The air conditioner vented just on the other side of the archway, and she yipped and jumped aside as the cold blast hit her damp skin. Her carefully balanced load slipped, and she instinctively made a grab for it. The towel fell to the floor.

"Is anything wrong, Emma?"

Emma jumped again and glanced over the railing. She gulped, her heart thumping erratically. Max and Dixie were just inside the front door, and he'd just finished unharnessing her. "Uh, n-no Max. Th-the air conditioner . . . I mean it's cold . . . I . . ." Oh, Lord! she thought. Standing stark naked in front of the sexy man who'd occupied every thought for days, and she blithered like an idiot. Why worry? He couldn't see her. "What could be wrong?" She moistened suddenly dry lips and bent toward the fallen towel but couldn't figure out how to pick it up. She pulled everything precariously under one arm and began to inch the other to the towel.

She heard footsteps on the stairs. After a quick, harried glance toward the towel, she decided it wasn't worth it. What if he ran into her? What if she dropped everything else? She began to edge toward her door.

"I don't know, Emma. Is the house still standing? Fire, flood, famine?"

"Of course not." Stop talking! she yelled silently. Her body gave her all sorts of incredible sensations, warming places she'd almost forgotten existed until Max had entered her life. Quivering excitement in the pit of her stomach brought on a full-scale attack of goose bumps. It's nerves, she told herself, just nerves.

"Then, what is it?"

"Nothing."

"You've been awfully quiet the last couple of days."

"I can be as quiet as a sinner on Sunday when I want to be, Max." Please, she prayed. Please let him stop at the archway so he doesn't trip on that damned towel!

He tripped on the top step, and she exclaimed in concern and stepped toward him.

"Don't touch me!" he said with a growl. He caught his balance on the banister and continued his journey. "I just counted wrong. Happens all the time." He was furious, Emma could see it in his face, and she felt as if he'd slapped her. "I'll be working tonight, but I'll be down to make dinner as soon as I change."

Max paused in the archway, his embarrassed cursing forgotten as her scent suddenly rolled over him, transporting him to a hot, moist jungle. He could almost hear the strident cries of the birds and feel the sword-edged grass under his hands. A panther crouched in those grasses, emerald eyes burning with unslaked hunger, waiting for its prey to move closer.

With an effort he forced the image back. "I hope you left the bathroom as you found it, Emma. I dislike cleaning up other people's messes."

"I borrowed a couple of towels," she said stiffly, "but otherwise it's neat as a schoolteacher's bun. And as for dinner, *I* will be down as soon as I dress." With that Emma spun into her room and slammed the door behind her.

Max's heart thudded into his chest. Dress. Not "change," "dress." He was paralyzed with the sharp flush of heat her little slip caused in his body, mesmerized by visions of glowing emerald cat eyes.

Or was her comment some little game, an erotic tease to his one darkened sense?

His body cooled even as his mind rebelled at the thought. Emma wasn't like that, he told himself with a surprising feeling of tender emotion. During the past days he'd been amazed at the speed with which she had adapted to his routine, instinctively, it seemed. Though he'd accused her, it was unfairly, because he'd never found a single thing out of place, something most sighted people would have found difficult. Yet she'd never complained. She wasn't the type to take advantage like some people he'd known. She was blatantly honest.

Wasn't she?

He involuntarily stepped toward her room, feeling as lost as he had those first few months after the accident, as if some necessary tie to reality had vanished. Then his foot nudged into something soft, and he reached down to pick it up. A damp towel, his senses told him. Filled with that unique fragrance. It cleared his fuzzy mind.

What was he doing? Standing there like some idiot, doubting himself, feeling the awkwardness he'd sworn never to feel again.

"Damn you, Emma," he muttered, and strode toward his room. He clutched the towel and wished it were her neck he was wringing. "I will not let you do this to me!"

But if Emma was as honest as he thought, then that would mean she was really—

He caught himself before he ran into his door.

Friday morning the radio weatherman cheerfully predicted temperatures in the low hundreds. The air conditioner gave a wheezing gasp and died. Max burned the toast, and Dixie threw up on the carpet.

It went downhill from there.

The muggy, hot atmosphere without the air conditioner was as nothing compared to the tense silence that permeated the house. Finally Emma said, "I'm going to decant the oil."

"Good," Max said shortly. "We're due at the lab tomorrow morning."

"And you'll dance afterward, right?" She attempted a laugh, but it came out sounding suspiciously like a sob. "The beginning of the end, Max. Your ordeal will soon be over."

She spun on her heel and missed Max's pain-filled expression.

Downstairs Emma scooped the mucusy mess out of the oil bath and slammed it into a nearby trash can with enough force to splatter it against the sides. Her heart swelled heavy in her chest, but she fought her silly tears. It was for the best, she told herself. Max didn't need her; he hadn't given one inch. She'd have been better off in prison. At least then she wouldn't have to see Max every day. She wouldn't have his tawny eyes haunt her sleep. She wouldn't have her body awaken every morning burning with unnamed longing.

In a few days this nightmare would be over. She'd have the money to save her home, and Max would be out of her life forever.

And she wanted it as badly as he did.

"How much longer?"

Emma glanced up from her task. Max stood stiffly on the stairs, defiant and proud, and all she could think about was how tightly his jeans hugged the contours of his thighs, how his tumbled golden hair begged for her fingers to touch it. She looked away. "A couple of minutes. As soon as I finish getting the big pieces out, I'll pour it through this cheesecloth-lined funnel into the flask, and that will be that."

"Just don't blow up anything."

Emma's hand slipped on the ceramic dish, and she cursed. "Don't worry, no fire, famine, or flood."

Max frowned, the fleeting thought that she'd lost her accent failing to pierce the emptiness that had opened inside of him. Nothing he had done had erased her from his mind or his house. No matter how hard he tried, she'd insinuated herself into every nook and cranny of his life, and he didn't know how to combat that.

She threatened him somehow, and he didn't know why. "Well," he said with forced heartiness. "By Christmas you'll be sitting on top of the world. What are you going to do with your first check, after, of course, you finish your mysterious project."

"I'll travel, I guess. As far from St. Louis as possib—"

She cut herself off with a gasp, and Max heard something crash to the floor. His stomach clenched, and he took an involuntary step toward her. "What happened? What's wrong?"

"Don't touch me," she said. "I dropped the bowl. Happens all the time."

Shards slammed into metal, and Max went cold. Her voice sounded familiar. He couldn't quite place it, but it stabbed through him like a hot knife. "Are you hurt?"

She gave a hysterical little giggle. "Me? I'm invulnerable, Max. No weakness here." Her activity ceased. "Did you just say our first check won't come until Christmas?"

"Of course. I thought you understood that." He frowned in confusion. "The—the market testing takes only a couple of weeks, but the ad campaign, the retail orders, everything takes time. I'm rushing it as it is, usually we work for at least a year on a new fragrance." He gasped. "And you don't have that time, do you?" He stepped to the bottom of the stairs. "Dammit, woman, I'll lend you the money! I'll give you the damn money!"

"I don't want your 'damn' money, Max. I want nothing from you! Do you understand? Nothing!" She groaned. "You don't understand, do you? But of course you don't, how could you? You have absolutely no concept of what it's like to have others depending on you, do you? Because you don't let anyone get that close! You shut yourself up in this house and chase off anyone who tries to get anywhere near you because then they might see that you're human after all!" She huffed. "Well, let me tell you something, Max, *I* don't need you. I don't need anyone! I'm perfectly capable of handling anyone or anything without your so-called help. I don't want your charity!"

With that she brushed past him and pounded up the stairs.

Max clutched the wooden rail, numb. Now he knew why Emma had sounded so familiar. She'd been as distant as Mars, as cold and unyielding as a glacier. He gulped convulsively.

She'd sounded just like him.

Six

Slumping to her bed, Emma fought her tears. After all she'd gone through, the work, the worry, the unbearable tension between her and Max, she'd failed anyway. She'd done everything wrong from the day she'd set foot in St. Louis.

And she'd lashed out at Max. All he'd wanted to do was help, but, of course, her pride wouldn't let him. Thanks to her damnable pride, the Machlens would lose the island. Thanks to her conviction that she and she alone could save it, she'd sealed their fate. Because of her stiff-necked independence, she couldn't ask for the help she so desperately needed.

A cold wave of realization froze the blood in her veins. Her words to Max echoed in her mind.

"Oh, no," she whispered. "Oh, no."

Her hand flew to her mouth, and her throat tightened. Oh, Lord, what had she done? How could she ever have thought him cold and unfeeling when all he'd ever done was protect himself? She of all people should have understood that!

Her eyes blurred, and shame flushed her cheeks. Max had challenged the world and won, achieving a success many would deem impossible. Yet he had gone along with her antics, had invited her into his home, though she knew how he felt about her. He wasn't some overbearing egotist, he was a courageous man battling odds that most would consider their worst nightmare.

What had she done? How could she ever make it up to him?

She couldn't. She could only apologize, then she'd pack her bags. There was no other alternative. Her stomach twisted in knots at the thought of leaving, of hurting him. She'd really done it this time.

Lost in her thoughts, she didn't hear the door handle turn. A whisper of sound made her look up as a white rose poked through, followed by Max's hand waving it back and forth. She jumped to her feet, her eyes wide.

"Truce?" came Max's voice from behind the door.

Emma gaped at the flower, unable to say a word. What was going on? she thought numbly. He should have stormed up demanding an apology. Instead, he offered peace?

"Emma?" he called. "Are you in there?"

"Y-yes, I—I . . ." Her throat closed on her words, but Max swung the door open and stepped into the room, smiling hesitantly. His blond hair was touseled, his unfocused amber eyes uncertain. He held the trembling rose in front of him.

"I, uh, didn't have a white flag. Will this do?"

Emma's tears spilled over to her cheeks, but she ignored them, ignored the possible meaning of his gesture.

"I'm sorry," he said.

"I'm sorry," she whispered at the same time.

His smile collapsed into concern. "Oh, Emma." He closed the gap between them, his searching hands finding her easily, his arms closing around her. "I've been a real bastard, haven't I?"

"You didn't do anything!" she said with a gasp. She wanted to resist his arms, she wanted to deny the comfort he offered, but she couldn't. Her bones seemed to melt, and her head dropped to his shoulder, nestling into the warm terry robe as if it belonged there. "At least nothing that I wasn't doing too. I—I can't let you help me, but here I was madder'n a wet hen because you wouldn't let me help you!" She attempted a poor chuckle. His arms tightened protectively, and her heart dropped to her toes. "It was a low blow, and I had no right to talk to you like that. I just can't get my foot out of my mouth around you."

"Shh." Max felt his throat burn. He was prepared for anger and indignation, not this. Her shoulders trembled with her tears, and she felt so fragile in his arms, as if the slightest wind would blow her away. But he knew she was strong, stronger than any woman he'd ever known. "I'm the one who should apologize. I never realized how I sounded to everybody else. Lord! I'm amazed no one has shot me down before."

"How could they?" she said in a choked voice.

He chuckled, as much to calm himself as her. "I never gave anyone a chance, huh?"

"That's not what I meant!"

"I know, Emma. I've never asked for any special favors because I'm blind, but I've been getting them nonetheless, haven't I? I just couldn't admit it." He drew her away and framed her face in his palms as the rose slid to the floor, forgotten. He ached with her pain, especially since he knew he was at fault.

Resisting the urge to drop a kiss on her lips, he turned to the dresser and fiddled with the various jars and bottles as he spoke. "I didn't stop to try to understand what you were feeling. I could only think how opposite we are. I didn't want to see the similarities. Pride is something I can understand, Emma. Believe me, I do."

The silence following his soft admission stretched. "Why are you telling me this?" she asked finally.

"I'm not sure." He abandoned the bottles and

turned, rubbing the scar on his forehead. "I'm not making excuses, at least I don't want to. I don't want your pity either."

"None was offered."

"I know," he whispered. He stepped toward her, reaching up to gently touch her face. "From the first day I met you I knew that. I guess I wanted to make sure nothing had changed." Her cheeks were wet, and he felt another tear roll onto his thumb. He groaned, his heart twisting. "Don't cry, Emma. I don't need your tears. I—I need your understanding."

"Me?" Her voice was a breathless, trembly whisper of sound. "Why me?"

"Because—because you make me see something in myself that I've never seen before. And I don't think I like me very much."

"I like you," she whispered.

Her breath warmed his cheek, and he suddenly realized her arms had traveled around his waist. Her body pressed against him, her scent wreathed him with a strange sense of peace that was at distinct odds with his growing arousal. He knew her mouth was mere inches from his, framed by his thumbs. Of their own accord his fingers slid into her hair while his thumbs stroked the contours of her lips. He felt the moment her breathing changed, felt the sharp thud of her heartbeat that echoed his own. He tilted her head and bent toward her, pulled by a wistful yearning for something . . . something.

Their lips brushed in a promise of ecstasy that sent him reeling. But he halted, swallowing convulsively. His mouth went dry. "I, uh . . ." Unable to pin down his vague panic, he pulled away from her and dropped his hands to his side. "Emma, I—I know you're in trouble, and I want to help. You need money. I want to draw up a contract with your company to develop an entire line based on Chameleon. Bath powder, body oil, the works."

She gasped. "Max, I can't let you do that!"

"Of course you can!"

"You've already arranged for production to begin before the results are even in! I haven't even finished distilling the essence I need for a lousy test batch. You can't risk that kind of investment before you know how the perfume will do!"

He clenched his fists. "Then tell me, Emma. Tell me why you need the money, and maybe we can figure something out."

Emma drew a shuddering breath. Lord, she wanted to trust him. He had allowed her a glimpse of intense vulnerability, but it was so hard to let him have the same look. Especially as he'd shut down again.

"It's nothing I can't handle," she said.

"Don't lie to me, Emma."

"I don't lie."

"Dammit!" He raked his fingers through his hair. "You are so stubborn! Can't you admit that maybe, just maybe, this is beyond even your remarkable capabilities?"

Tears stung her eyes. After his confession she'd wanted only to hold him. Now she wanted to be held. And that was silly. "I don't want your pity either," she whispered.

He grinned lopsidedly. "None was offered."

"And I don't want this—this thing between us to cloud your judgment."

He stiffened. "I've never been distracted by physical attraction, Emma."

It was more than physical attraction, she thought dazedly, though that was certainly part of it. Her whole body burned with a fire he had ignited. Her breasts ached with the need for his touch, her heartbeat raced with just the memory of his mouth hovering over hers. She couldn't even raise any anger at words that should have hurt her by their offhandedness. Max was protecting himself the only way he knew how.

She bent to pick up the fallen rose and breathed deeply of its fragrance. Something was happening to her, something awesome and a little scary. She stood on the edge of some vast precipice, and Max had stopped her from falling into it. Why? Why had he denied her that final step? And did she really want to take it?

She squared her shoulders. The only way to find out was to leap headlong, to stop fighting it. And that began with trust. "In less than sixty days Machlen Island goes on the auction block, Max. Unless I can raise enough money to pay the taxes."

"Taxes?" He frowned. "Emma, I thought you said your business was doing well. How could something like that happen?"

"It is doing well. Under normal circumstances we'd be fine." She sighed and sank to the bed. "The trouble started about a year ago. Someone began to set fires on the island. Just little ones. Warning us."

He crossed the room and sat next to her. "Warning," he repeated, puzzled. "Is someone trying to run you out of business?"

Emma's hand clenched around the fragile blossom she still held, and she stared blankly at the crushed petals. "Not out of business, off the island. Have you ever heard of Hilton Head? Fripp?"

He nodded. "Sure. They're little islands developers have made over into resorts for the rich and as meccas for tourists." He gasped. "Fripp is near Beaufort, right?"

"Give that man a cigar," she muttered.

"And developers are after Machlen."

"That's what we think. They approached us to sell several years ago, but it's our home, Max. Our home." She laid the rose gently on her pillow. "The fires didn't work, so a few weeks later someone started poaching. We have a herd of rare deer on the island. We lost three before we decided to give our dogs run of the place. But the worst came about a month ago."

"When your company wrote to me."

"Yes. We had a hurricane a few years back, and a tree came down on part of the house. We rebuilt it. Last month we were notified that we had made an improvement and that our property had been reassessed at its current market value."

"Which had escalated drastically because of all the ritzy developments in the area."

"Exactly." She sighed. "We don't know who began this battle, and we don't know who contacted the state, or if they were bribed. We just know that we have a big chunk of money due."

"Can't you borrow—"

"No!" Her stomach tightened. "We've never borrowed money in our lives! One of the reasons I started this company was that—" She bit her lip.

"Yes?"

She glanced up, surprised to find understanding on his face. He made no judgments. "My parents are proud people, Max. Most of us have college educations thanks to them, but they wouldn't let us give them anything in return. When the farm failed, the only way any of us could repay them was to find another source of income. Island Organics is it."

"I see. Now I know where you get it from." His expression softened. "You're an amazing woman, you know that?"

Her breath caught in her throat. She felt it again, the tugging sensation that seemed to come from his soul, and she leaned toward him. She didn't understand any of it, but she wanted everything from him. "Max," she whispered, and reached to touch him.

He lost his smile and stood abruptly, grabbing the bedpost as if to steady himself. "I think I have a reasonable compromise, if you'll listen."

Emma dropped her hand, stinging from his rejection. She wanted everything, and he wanted nothing. "I think you should buy it outright, as I offered in the first place."

He waved away her suggestion. "Let's not go back to that, all right? I'm not going to take advantage of your difficulty for my gain."

"Are you sure you're not a Machlen?" she asked with a hesitant smile.

He shrugged, his brow furrowed in thought. "What if I advanced you the money based on projected sales?"

"We don't have any projections yet."

"I do. In my mind."

She hesitated. Trust was a very fragile thing, she found. But she couldn't allow her personal feelings to keep her from the important issues. "All right, Max. But I'm staying to make sure everything goes right. I won't have you losing money on this investment." She stood. "I'll move into a hotel immediately."

"No!" He turned away from her. "I mean, that's not necessary, Emma. We're mature adults. I'm sure we can occupy the same house without either of us losing our objectivity."

She opened her mouth to protest, but he cut her off.

"Besides, you were released into my custody, remember? It's my duty to keep you off the streets of St. Louis and away from the law-abiding citizens." He turned and held out a hand. "Friends?"

She frowned, wondering what he wanted. One minute he was trying like mad to get her out, the next he was finding excuses for her to stay. It was very confusing, but she grasped his hand tightly. "Friends."

"Good."

The air around them shivered with unspoken words, suppressed emotions. Max realized he hadn't dropped her hand, that the friendly handshake had the disturbing overtones of a caress.

He let go abruptly and spun away. "I'm going for my swim. You're welcome to use the pool, but you'd better hurry. I'm hungry."

He didn't wait for an answer but stumbled from the room, feeling for the rail. His urge to flee erased any embarrassment he may have felt, but even that knowledge failed to pierce his confusion. Why had he told her she could stay? Why hadn't he stuck her in a hotel, away from him?

He rushed to change into his trunks, then went downstairs, slowing only when he bumped against the screen door. He threw it open and rushed outside into the already stifling heat. He felt for the edge and depth markers of the pool with his foot, then dove cleanly into the cool water, pushing himself immediately into a fast stroke as he surfaced.

The water shocked his surprisingly overheated body, calming his violent need for her. Friendship was much more important and more lasting than desire. He knew that from experience. Emma's opinion mattered, and he didn't want to mess it up. He didn't want anything out of gratitude. He didn't want anything.

Maybe that's why he'd asked her to stay. To test his willpower. He knew he couldn't take advantage of her in an emotional moment. And he certainly couldn't take advantage of her in his own home.

No matter how much he wanted to.

Emma stared after him a moment, then decided she wouldn't let him off so easily. Something had happened between them, and she wasn't about to run from it.

Maybe Max was just as confused as she.

She squared her shoulders and changed into her turquoise bikini.

When she entered the kitchen, Dixie greeted

her with excitement, running back and forth between her and the door like a puppy. Emma
laughed as she slid it open and watched the dog
bound out and run straight for the pool. Dixie
barked and launched herself into the water with a
tremendous splash. Emma couldn't help giggling
as Max cursed good-naturedly at the sudden
shower.

"Did I forget you, girl?" She heard him laugh as
she walked across the warm flagstones. He was in
the deep end, and his head bobbed under the
water as Dixie paddled over to him. He swam
along the bottom, surfacing in the shallow end
and calling his dog to redirect her. It appeared to
be a game of tag.

Emma caught her breath. His fair hair lay plastered against his skull, almost brown in the water. His skimpy red swimsuit clung to him, outlining
and emphasizing every contour. He was magnificent.

A warm tingling spread upward from her toes
right to her scalp. She wanted to touch him so
badly that she clenched her fists at her sides. She
couldn't remember ever feeling this attracted to a
man, this drawn.

But she had to find out why he had closed
himself off. She had to know if the attraction was
one-sided, because if she stood any chance at all
with him, she wanted it. This eternal dance around
their emotions was driving her crazy.

And if he felt nothing? Her mouth firmed. She
would cross that bridge if and when she came to
it.

Running to the edge of the deep end, she dove,
slipping into the water like an otter. She surfaced, gasping, so close to Max that she could feel
his body's heat. He stood frozen in the shallow
end, a strange expression of shock on his face.
Emma reached out and slapped his chest. "You're
it!" she cried, and jumped away before she could

give into the other urge, her disconcerting need to rub her cheek against him.

Max's eyes narrowed. "Dixie, out!" he called, a reluctant smile twitching the corners of his mouth. "Leave me a clear field."

The dog splashed to the stairs, climbed out, shook herself, and plopped down at the edge to watch. Emma giggled, and Max cocked his head. "So, Miss Smarty-Pants, you think you can hide from me, huh?"

Emma ran out of footing as she backed slowly into the deep end, but she breathed a small prayer of thanks. She had him laughing again, and that relieved her more than she'd thought it would.

Silence fell as Max stood, waiting, listening, and Emma carefully treaded water. No, it wasn't quite silent, she realized suddenly. Water lapped the blue tile softly, the sound of a distant power mower hummed faintly in the humid air, and a strident car horn made her jump. The world was a very noisy place.

And smells! The chlorine barely masked the scent of damp, steaming grass, hot earth, and wet dog.

Is this what Max "sees"?

Her mind snapped back as Max moved toward her. His face reflected the intensity of his concentration, and Emma sobered, sensing it had become a very serious game indeed. She scissored away from him as he neared, and he lunged, almost but not quite touching her. She froze again while Max treaded water. Imperceptibly she let her moving arms and legs ease her back toward shallower water.

His head turned as she touched bottom. Her body slid up and out of the water, and she tiptoed toward the other end of the pool. Max slowly swam toward her. She changed direction, angling to her right, and Max continued swimming toward her last position. Her feet touched cold tile, and she stifled a tiny gasp. Max was walking now, his body aimed at a place just to her left. As he neared, she lowered herself back into the water.

His arm shot out and touched her head. "Gotcha!" he cried, a triumphant grin splitting his face. Emma shrieked and shot up, pushing an armload of water into his face. He sputtered and splashed back.

The battle was on, each combatant throwing almost as much water onto the patio as on each other. Dixie ran along the edge of the pool, barking her encouragement. Max ducked his head and worked his way toward Emma, finally catching her tormenting arms at the wrists. "Now, now," he chided. "Mustn't be a sore loser."

"Pure luck," she said as primly as she could under her giggles.

"Not luck," he told her. "Currents and your very noisy dripping."

Emma groaned. "Superman unmasked."

"Not quite," he said. "I'm not exactly the X-ray vision type, you know."

Her laughter slowed as she realized Max hadn't released her. "I won't splash anymore. I promise."

"And you never lie, do you?" he asked softly as he dropped her arms. A smile chased across his face and was gone, leaving a strange confusion that Emma longed to wipe away. "You just refuse to tell."

He shouldn't have touched her, she thought dimly. His hands wreaked havoc with her body, accelerating her pulse to an alarming rate. Her breasts felt heavy, swelling against the skimpy suit. The water ebbed and flowed softly around them, brushing her thighs like cool silk.

Her eyes were drawn to his face, to the smile that suddenly faded, to the unfocused eyes that suddenly darkened. His fingers moved on her shoulders, stroking her sensitive skin, and she had the oddest feeling that he saw her better than anyone ever had.

Never in her wildest dreams had she imagined she could ever feel this way. She had known only surface emotions before. Max touched her soul as no one ever had. He made her feel fragile, and feminine, and . . .

"You're beautiful, Emma Machlen. I've never met anyone so beautiful."

His husky voice sent her heart leaping to her throat. And his mouth, when it settled lightly on hers, sent an aching spiral of sweet pain deep into the very core of her being.

Her lips parted. Her eyes fluttered closed. His tongue darted to her lips, teasing her, taunting her, initiating a different game of tag that made her senses spin. She pressed against him, her breasts brushing the wet roughness of his chest, fitting into the hard contours of his body like a second skin. Exquisite agony flooded her, shattering her, opening a vast emptiness that she knew only Max could fill.

Max spun into mindlessness, his senses reeling with the feel of Emma's willow-slender body pressed against his. He savored the sweet dampness of her mouth as if it were a fine wine, with forbidden sips that only tantalized and hinted at its true, heady pleasure. His body throbbed to a hard, primal rhythm. He wanted more of her, all of her, as he had for so long.

She whispered something against his lips, but he couldn't hear for the pounding in his ears. His hands left her shoulders, sliding over her damp skin until his thumbs touched the edge of her suit. He groaned and pressed his mouth to hers, no longer sipping but drinking deeply, plumbing the sweet depths with his tongue as his fingers slid up the narrow string to the nape of her neck. The wet knot was stubborn, but with a jerk it came free. He slid the strings downward until he felt the soft rise of her breasts.

His mouth left hers then, trailing kisses down

her arched neck to the hollow of her throat, lapping the tiny puddle there. His fingers followed the curve of her breast until they found the hard, hot buds of her nipples. She gasped as he rolled them gently in his fingers, and he felt his manhood strain against the restricting suit. Her hands circled his neck, guiding him downward. His hands moved to her waist, lifting her against him, fitting her softness against his hard body perfectly, driving him mad with wanting her as he licked and sucked her faintly fragrant skin. His tongue explored the valley between her breasts, but it wasn't enough. He wanted more. Lord, he wanted to take her nipple in his teeth, then sheath himself inside her hot body until they both exploded in an uncontrollable maelstrom. . . .

With a shuddering sigh he stopped. He couldn't do it, not there, not then. Not ever.

"What's wrong?" she whispered. Her voice echoed his anguish, but he could only shake his head and bury his face in the sweet curve of her neck, his arms tightening around her as he fought for control of his body. There was no more panic, and that disturbed him as much as the fear had. Reluctantly he lowered her back into the water and caught the floating straps of her suit, retying them quickly before he lost what semblance of sanity he had regained.

"I can't, Emma. I'm sorry."

"Why?"

Trust Emma to be blunt when it suited her, he thought with a pained laugh. "If I say I don't know, will you leave it alone?"

"For now," she whispered.

The water moved around him as she swam away. He wanted to call her back. He wanted to erase the ache he had heard in her one simple syllable. But he needed the physical distance she had set.

"You don't make any sense, Max. Do you know that?"

"Just stop trying to make us more than friends, Emma."

"Just stop trying to make us any less," she countered.

Blithely disregarding the truth in her statement, he groped for the ladder and heaved himself from the water, searching for the towel that was draped over the lounge. A change of subject was definitely in order. "Are you going to have to send for some more barometer grass?"

"No."

He jumped. Emma was right behind him. Lord, she moved like a breath of air! He turned and defensively stuck out the towel. She took it, and he tried not to imagine her rubbing it over her wet skin, along every curve of her silken body.

"There's more than enough essence for the test batch," she said. "I ruined only a small part of it."

He paused. "And you? You're not a prisoner, no matter what you think. Would you like to go out sight-seeing with Adam?"

"No, thank you." She hesitated. "But I'd like to go with you. Isn't that what friends do?"

"Me?" He thought of the implications and clenched his fists. Why not? Emma deserved it after all he'd put her through. "Sure." He pushed his fears far away. "Tomorrow, all right?"

"Great!"

"Do you have anything in mind?" he asked, forcing a casual tone he was far from feeling.

"You mean besides blowing up your stillroom and seducing you?"

He did his best to glare at her. "For St. Louis."

She giggled at his attempt and abandoned her attitude. "Yes. I want to see the Arch."

"The Arch it is," he said with a smile, then turned toward the house.

Emma watched him walk away from her, more confused than ever at his attitude, his rapid turnabouts. She wanted to understand him, she wanted to have more than a tiny peek at the world as he saw it. The gentle soul she'd first glimpsed was there; it would be up to her to unlock it. Because Cissy was right. She'd jumped in with both feet this time. And one thing shined with crystal clarity in her mind.

She was falling in love with him.

Seven

"Ready?"

Emma nodded to Tony, the squat, bald-headed chemist. The fluorescent lighting gave his face an unhealthy green glow, but his expression was placid. He flipped a switch, and the bewildering machine on the lab counter began to hum. Surreptitiously she tucked her hands into the pockets of her white coat and crossed her fingers.

"You're absolutely sure you gave him the correct amounts?"

She glanced over at Max, wondering if the anxiety that tinged his voice was for his company or her personally. They had declared a tremulous, platonic peace since they'd left the pool, and Emma had vowed patience. They would remain friends, at least for a while, if it killed her. And if her highly erotic dream of the previous night was any indication, it would. But, she told herself brutally, the project came first. Only her concern for her family could keep her from throwing herself into his arms and kissing him senseless. "I'm very precise, Max," she said with more confidence than she felt. "Just hope your computer is."

Tony inserted her last vial of barometer grass essence into its designated slot alongside the sixteen others, and placed a bottle carefully underneath the spigot. Emma added a prayer, just in case.

"Here we go," he said, and punched a command into his terminal.

In a disgustingly short period of time the tiny flask was full. Emma let out a breath she didn't even know she'd been holding and picked the container up with trembling fingers. Her heartbeat raced as she dabbed a drop on her wrist and brought it to her nose. To her outward pleasure and her secret astonishment it smelled exactly as it should. "That's it," she said cheerfully, and gave the bottle to Tony, who left the room with Max's instructions to send it to the marketing firm in Los Angeles.

"May I?" Max asked.

Emma placed her hand in Max's, and he sniffed her wrist. A tiny shiver played over her body. Friendship was highly overrated, she decided. "Well?" she asked breathlessly.

Max froze, then he smiled before releasing her arm. "Smells like a cross between a florist's shop and a bakery."

She laughed. "Three days from now you won't even recognize it."

"It amazes me that an odorless essence can pull that jumble of scents together and allow each to emerge in a different order."

"That's its subtlety," she said softly. "It's brilliant in its natural setting, coloring rapidly with the atmosphere around it. It's invisible to the senses when placed in another environment, yet pervasive when surrounded by stronger scents. Because of its unexpectedness, its change brings out the best in everything."

His smile faded. "Does it? Does it really?"

"Yes, Max," she whispered. "Sometimes all it takes is a shift in perspective."

He swallowed hard. "You—"

"Sorry I'm late!" called Adam as he rushed in. "Is it over?"

Max stepped away and smiled brightly at his friend. Emma glared at him. He raised his brows in inquiry and winked at her.

"You missed—quite a bit," said Max.

Adam's blue eyes darted from Max to Emma and back again. He shrugged. "I was busy. The check is gone—you're broke, by the way, Max"— they chuckled—"and Emma, I have yet another of these endless contracts for you to sign." He handed her a sheaf of papers.

She glanced over it. "Exclusive rights to the extraction process?"

Adam nodded. "It's not only the scent itself, but the barometer grass that makes it so valuable. You told me it grows on your island and a few of the surrounding islands, but that it isn't an endangered species, right?"

"Right," she said cautiously.

"That means any company could get its hands on it, and duplicate its remarkable essence. And they'll try, believe me. Once this hits the market, it will cause the biggest stir since the discovery of ambergris."

"Then the fixative is the real potential gold mine," she muttered.

"Adam," Max said, "I think I hear the wheels turning."

"I have a big mouth, don't I?" Adam grinned, totally unrepentant.

Emma thought it over quickly and handed the contract back to Adam, unsigned. "Sorry, Max. You own one scent. I think I'll hold on to the rest."

"You're not going to believe this," he said gently. "But I'm trying to protect your interests. We have the security setup to prevent its theft."

Her breath caught in her throat. "I believe you, Max. I do. But only three people really know the

IF YOU LOVE ROMANCE...
THEN YOU'RE READY TO BE "LOVESWEPT"!

Mail this heart today! (see inside)

LOVESWEPT INVITES YOU
TO OPEN YOUR HEART
TO LOVE
AND WE'LL GIVE YOU
6 FREE BOOKS
A FREE LIGHTED MAKEUP CASE
AND MUCH MORE

OPEN YOUR HEART TO LOVE.. YOU'LL BE LOVESWEPT WITH THIS FREE OFFER!

HERE'S WHAT YOU GET:

1. **FREE!** SIX NEW LOVESWEPT NOVELS! You get 6 beautiful stories filled with passion, romance, laughter, and tears...exciting romances to stir the excitement of falling in love... again and again.

2. **FREE!** A BEAUTIFUL MAKEUP CASE WITH A MIRROR THAT LIGHTS UP! What could be more useful than a makeup case with a mirror that lights up*? Once you open the tortoise-shell finish case, you have a choice of brushes...for your lips, your eyes, and your blushing cheeks.

*(batteries not included)

3. **SAVE!** MONEY-SAVING HOME DELIVERY! Join the Loveswept at-home reader service and we'll send you 6 new novels each month. You always get 15 days to preview them before you decide. Each book is yours for only $2.09 — a savings of 41¢ per book.

4. **BEAT THE CROWDS!** You'll always receive your Loveswept books before they are available in bookstores. You'll be the first to thrill to these exciting new stories.

BE LOVESWEPT TODAY — JUST COMPLETE, DETACH AND MAIL YOUR FREE-OFFER CARD.

FREE–LIGHTED MAKEUP CASE!
FREE–6 LOVESWEPT NOVELS!

- NO OBLIGATION
- NO PURCHASE NECESSARY

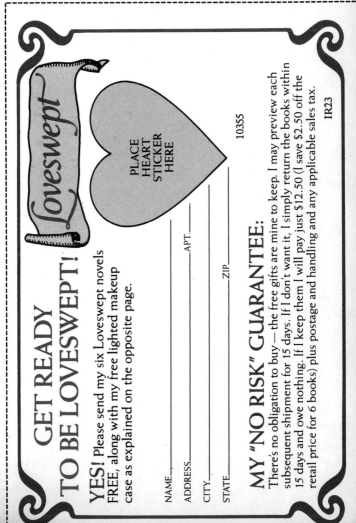

GET READY TO BE LOVESWEPT!

YES! Please send my six Loveswept novels FREE, along with my free lighted makeup case as explained on the opposite page.

NAME_____

ADDRESS_____APT._____

CITY_____

STATE_____ZIP_____

MY "NO RISK" GUARANTEE:

There's no obligation to buy — the free gifts are mine to keep. I may preview each subsequent shipment for 15 days. If I don't want it, I simply return the books within 15 days and owe nothing. If I keep them I will pay just $12.50 (I save $2.50 off the retail price for 6 books) plus postage and handling and any applicable sales tax.

IR23

10355

Loveswept

PLACE HEART STICKER HERE

REMEMBER!

- The free books and gift are mine to keep!
- There is no obligation!
- I may preview each shipment for 15 days!
- I can cancel anytime!

NO POSTAGE
NECESSARY
IF MAILED
IN THE
UNITED STATES

BUSINESS REPLY MAIL

FIRST-CLASS MAIL   PERMIT NO. 2456   HICKSVILLE, N.Y.

POSTAGE WILL BE PAID BY ADDRESSEE

Loveswept

Bantam Books
P.O. Box 985
Hicksville, NY 11802-9827

entire process. Myself, my mother, and my sister Diana."

"And me. I was there, remember?"

"You were there, yes," she said with a dimpled grin. "But the key to the extraction process is the way it *looks* while it's being prepared, its color when it's finished."

Max's mouth worked, then he chuckled. "I think I've been outflanked."

"Neatly," said Adam.

"I do know enough of the initial preparation to make me dangerous, Emma. You know that."

"I know that," she whispered. "And I trust you to keep the secret." For a moment the air trembled between them with the implications of her statement.

His laughter died abruptly. "I will. I'll—" He swallowed. "I'll keep it locked away as tight as—as a—"

"Virgin on her wedding night?" supplied Adam.

The mood had broken. Emma groaned. "You have no flair for metaphors, you heathen! As tight as a parson in a brothel, as a housewife's diary. Get into the swing, Adam. You'll get it."

"Does everyone in your family talk as if they walked off the set of an old B movie?" asked Adam.

She shook her head. "Sorry, just me."

"An awesome gift," he said solemnly.

"It's something all right," Max agreed with a nod.

They left the laboratory in good spirits, and Adam asked Emma if she had any plans for the day.

"We're going to the Arch," she said.

"We?" His eyes opened wide. "As in you and Max?"

Max tensed. "Of course."

Adam whistled. "About this contract, Emma. Can we at least discuss exclusive rights to the essence?"

"We can discuss it," she said with a puzzled look at Max.

"Maybe Daniels Cosmetics should merge with Island Organics, Max. This lady may just wipe us off the map if we're not careful."

"It's a thought," Max said in an odd tone of voice as he and Emma walked down the hall. "It's definitely a thought."

As they drove down the elm-lined street, she studied Max through narrowed eyes. The sunlight and flickering shadows of the trees played hide-and-seek in his hair, firing it with red highlights one moment, darkening it ominously the next. It was almost as if two separate people sat beside her.

His posture was casual, which suited his tan slacks and open-throated polo shirt. Too casual, she decided as she watched him nervously fingering the cane in his lap. He offhandedly explained that his cane was better in confined spaces, and they'd left Dixie at home because she was too big to fit into the observation cars that traveled into the Arch. It made sense, but this forced calm didn't. In spite of his seeming indifference, she could see that the trip had made him clench up like . . . like a virgin on her wedding night.

"Would you like a cigarette and blindfold?" she asked with a grin.

"What?"

"You look as though you're about to face a fir-ing squad, Max."

He smiled, but it was a rather sickly smile. "It's too hot to get shot today."

Emma frowned. What was going on? "What do you think, Benno? Is this a good day for an execution?"

"A good day? *Nein*. It will rain, I think."

"And so ends that discussion," she muttered, and went back to contemplating the scenery.

They drove into the heart of St. Louis, maneuvering through streets clogged with traffic into a parking lot near the Mississippi River. As the engine ceased, Max reached into his pocket and pulled out dark glasses Emma couldn't remember ever seeing him wear before. He donned them quickly, almost distastefully, and exited the car. Benno opened her door, helped her out, and climbed back into the front seat. Max waited on the other side of the car, standing stiffly, and she strode to him quickly.

The voices echoed clearly in his mind. The sound of a crowd, of people talking, calling out, children laughing, a baby crying. He forced himself to concentrate on the here and now, not the disorienting echoes. He would do this, he told himself firmly. He'd driven Emma insane with her captivity. He owed her this.

He listened intently, finding the sound of the tugboats on the river. That would be his direction. And he would not reveal his fear to Emma. It was her day.

"Underneath is the Jefferson National Expansion Memorial," Max told her as they wended through the parking lot. "But now we simply call it all the Arch."

Emma glanced up to the graceful curve of steel that arced into the sky. She frowned and brought her gaze back to him. Her fingers itched to take his arm as he led the way to the walkway, but he'd become distant and unapproachable, and she could only wonder vaguely how he knew its location. As he paused to orient himself, his chin tilted up as if he'd steeled himself for some kind of ordeal. She glanced around.

Though it was early, the parking lot and grassy acreage surrounding the Arch were already crowded. Emma barely noticed the wide river practically at her feet, she hardly saw the showboats tied at the levee farther along, or the stately grace of the city beside her. She saw only the people around them.

What was it about them that upset Max? There were a few surreptitious glances in his direction, even an occasional blatant stare, but it was nothing that his fair good looks wouldn't cause under normal circumstances. His dark glasses and cane merely gave him a different quality. Did it threaten him?

"How about an Uzi and a gun belt?" she asked.

"Emma, as usual, I have absolutely no idea what you're talking about."

"You're girding your loins again. I thought you did that only when people broke into your house."

"Are we here to sight-see or psychoanalyze?"

She frowned. "I'm at your disposal, sir," she said, watching him closely. "Where to?"

The muscles of Max's back tensed, clearly outlined by the taut shirt as he squared his shoulders and turned into the light breeze. "This way," he said stiffly, and began along the sidewalk, his white cane tapping on the concrete as he swept it back and forth across his path, constantly cutting himself a swath through the crowd. Emma walked silently on his left as he hugged the right side of the path, following the tide of humanity to the base of the Arch.

He negotiated the steps down to a little museum at its foot, and she followed, certain of his direction but cringing inwardly. His discomfort was beginning to transmit itself to her, and she fought the urge to draw her veil. She was through hiding her head in the sand.

"Do you see a ticket line?" he asked.

Emma glanced around. "Yes."

"Where?"

Her jaw clenched. Of course he wouldn't ask her to lead him to it. "Straight ahead, about fifteen feet. There are fourteen people in line."

He nodded and walked forward, stopping when his cane hit a foot. A small towheaded child licking a strawberry ice cream cone stared up at Max

with wide eyes. Emma shifted her feet, regretting
this idea but determined to carry it through. Didn't
Max understand that people believed what they
saw, that the moment he'd put his mask in place
he'd opened himself to the kind of attention he
seemed determined to ignore?

"Mithter? Are your eyeth broke?"

"Tommy," said the woman beside him, obviously appalled at her son's question. "I'm sorry,
sir. You know how kids are."

Emma glanced at Max. She expected anger or
withdrawal. What she saw astonished her.

His face softened, and he squatted in front of
the child. "It's all right." He smiled. "What's your
name? Tommy?"

"Yeth," the boy whispered, his lip trembling at
his mother's reaction.

"Well, Tommy. My eyes *are* broken in a way. I
hurt them a long time ago, and now I can't see
with them. But that doesn't mean I can't see at
all."

Tommy frowned, puzzling it out. "Huh?" he
said finally.

Max stifled a chuckle. "How old are you?"

"Thith many." He held up a sticky hand and
showed four fingers.

Max touched it gently. "Four, huh? You're pretty
big for four."

"I am?" His eyes widened. "Hey, you thaw me?"

"Sort of." Max cocked his head. "Tommy, have
you ever played pin the tail on the donkey?"

He nodded enthusiastically. "At my brother'th
birthday party. I won!" he finished proudly.

"Remember when they covered your eyes? You
couldn't see the donkey, but you pinned him,
right? How did you do that?"

Tommy frowned again, then his face cleared.
"Oh!"

"That's how." He stood. "But we'll keep it our
secret, okay?"

"Okay."

The line moved forward, and Tommy's mother smiled at Max. "Thanks," she whispered. "That was nice of you."

They paid for their tickets and moved through the turnstile.

As Max fumbled for the correctly folded bills from his wallet, Emma wiped away a stray tear. "Yeah, Max," she whispered through a tight throat as he walked ahead. "That was nice of you."

They rode the observation car in silence. The disconcerting rocking sway of the seat made Emma a little nauseated as it climbed the slope inside the Arch, but it was his attitude that puzzled her the most. Once up, they exited, and Max drew her forward to a small window, one of many that lined the wall.

Her nausea and her half-answered questions about Max's behavior disappeared from her mind as she gazed downward, the entire city lying before her. "Oh, Max," she said. "It's beautiful."

Unconsciously she reached out, touching her fingers against the coolness of the glass as if she could flow into the city itself. Then, without really wondering why, she began to describe it.

"It's all spread out before us, Max. Like a crazy quilt inscribed with ribbons of gray satin, covered with children's toys from different centuries. . . ."

The buildings were a curious blend of old and new, from the garden rooftop of some hotel, to the towering skyscrapers of rectangular concrete, to the twisted spire of a church, to the green dome of a courthouse or city hall. Verdant parkland was bordered by stately edifices of a bygone era. Metal antennae that would blink dimly red at night perched incongruously on top of antique structures. All of it flowed from her eyes to her lips, while she barely paid attention to anything or anyone around her.

Max listened to her words, amazed at the vivid images she evoked. It was almost as if she had *become* the scenery, and his mind presented him with the city he'd nearly forgotten. A curious peace settled in his heart.

"St. Louis is the leader in urban renewal," Max told her softly when she paused in wonder. "At least, we like to think so. Do you see a rectangular building, a cap of stairs at the top?"

"Yes."

"That's part of Union Station. Some years ago it was falling into ruin. Now it's incredible—shops, a hotel, all meticulously restored to grandeur. I'd like to take you there."

"I'd love it," she said, but her voice sounded strained, even to her ears. Now that her near trance had disappeared, she wasn't sure she wanted to go anywhere with Max when it was such a trial for him. "What's that building right in front? It looks like the Capitol building in Washington."

"The old Courthouse," he said. "Two of the five Dred Scott trials were argued there."

"And is that Busch Stadium?" she asked, glancing over to a huge oval. Obviously it was, but she wanted to keep him talking.

"Yep. The busiest place in town." He smiled. "You probably know what a baseball-crazy town St. Louis is."

"I've heard. Do you like baseball?"

He shrugged, and Emma watched him closely. "I used to go all the time," he said, "but I haven't been to a game in years."

Since I went blind was his unspoken comment, and a vague plan began to form in her mind as he continued telling her about the massive renovation that had been going on in his beloved town. She listened and watched his face light up as he related the information.

Suddenly the floor under her feet moved, shattering the mood, and she gripped his arm convulsively. "Max!" she said with a gasp. "We're falling!" Several other people cried out as the Arch began to sway. With an odd, quavery chuckle, Max slid his arms around her and held her close, fitting his chin to the top of her head.

"A storm's blowing in," he told her softly, soothingly. "Just as Benno predicted. I don't like storms any more than the next person, but it'll break this heat wave. The old Arch can withstand tornadoes, honey. A little breeze won't topple it."

Emma couldn't speak past her suddenly tight throat. His gesture had been comforting, but the contact sent messages to her brain that had nothing to do with fear anymore. A scent, Max's own personal fragrance, swirled into her mind, wrapping it into the numbness she was beginning to know so well. Her pulse pounded in her ears, and she was aware of nothing but him. She swayed with something other than the wind, and her arms crept around him, holding him close.

His amusement faded, and she felt his own heart jump erratically. His arms tightened slowly, his fingers brushed her back in a tentative motion that sent ripples of pleasure coursing through her. Her heartbeat increased with his, pounding in sync, and the rest of the world disappeared as their bodies danced with a rhythm all their own.

She lifted her head from the cradle of his throat and tilted it up to him. The dark glasses hid any expression in his eyes, but his golden head bent toward her slowly. Watching him carefully, she fit her mouth to his as it touched her fleetingly. With a low groan his mouth returned, joining hers with unexpected hunger, setting every nerve ending instantly alight. Her eyes drifted closed, and her arms tightened around him.

His tongue darted out to hers, mating in an explosive union that only shadowed her real need.

She drew him into her, reveling in the taste of him, the feel of his hands stroking her body, of his hard arousal pressed into her. It was as if they were the only two people left on earth.

And she loved him.

Her own whimper of pleasure was unconscious, but it seemed to recall him to sanity. His mouth left hers, and he held her close, attempting to control his ragged breathing. Emma listened to his racing heartbeat and smiled, trembling. Her soul sang with the intensity of his reaction.

She opened her eyes, and the fantasy exploded. Standing on the other side of the Arch was a group of teenage girls. At her notice, they burst into a round of whispered giggles and averted their gazes. Max tensed.

"Let's get out of here," he whispered hoarsely, and Emma nodded. He released her quickly, leaving her strangely disoriented, and groped for the cane he had laid on the shelf below the viewports while he'd talked.

As Max moved back to the observation car, his icy cloak firmly around his shoulders again as he tapped his cane, Emma's vague plan became vividly clear.

Max treated the world as an enemy, something to battle. While Emma saw only beauty, Max saw obstacles. Some of his Jericho wall was down. Maybe a little lesson in camouflage would take care of the rest.

"Can we cut this short, Max? I have something I need to do."

His stiff nod was curiously defeated, but she didn't have a moment to worry about it. She had too much to do. It was time Maxwell Morgan learned a few things about independence.

Eight

"Is she back yet?"

Adam's frantic query and rush into the room came simultaneously with another deafening clap of thunder. Max flinched. Cold sweat beaded his brow, his hands clenched convulsively in Dixie's fur. The dog whimpered and licked his shaking hand. "No," he said, furious when his voice broke.

"My Lord, what's wrong with you? You're white as a sheet!"

Max tried to relax into his leather chair, he tried to appear unaffected, but thunder rolled again, and he trembled. "You really need lessons from Emma. Your metaphors are rather cliché, Adam."

"It's the storm," Adam whispered. "Lord, it's the storm!"

Max heard the clink of glass against glass, and then Adam pressed something into his hand. He drank automatically, the whiskey cauterizing his dry throat. He choked, but his hands stilled.

Damn! He felt like a fool.

"You weren't supposed to come over!" he said to his friend. "I just thought Emma might have run to you."

"Don't snarl at me, Max. I don't even know what this is all about. Why would she want to run?"

Max hesitated. "Do you remember the first time Shannon ever went out in public with me after the accident?"

"How could I forget? She bitched about it for weeks beforehand, telling you it was unhealthy to shut yourself up in the house, then dragged you all over town as if you couldn't do anything yourself." Adam gasped. "Is that what Emma did? You're lying!"

Max's throat tightened, and he gulped the alcohol again, shutting out the memory with the sound of the storm.

"Oh, hell, I'm sorry. I didn't mean to say that. I only meant she wouldn't do that."

"No, she didn't. She's—" He shook his head. "I meant afterward. Do you remember what happened after that?"

"Of course. Shannon decided your social standing wasn't worth your rigid control. You terrified her."

Max blinked. "That was blunt."

"But true, and you know it. Hell, Max, it had nothing to do with the accident. You shut down a long time ago. You just had a good excuse when you were blinded. Shannon dumped you—another excuse, by the way—and it didn't bother you at all. You—" Adam made a sound of discovery. "You think that's what Emma did. You think she turned tail after your little trip because she decided she couldn't live with you, is that it?"

"She didn't even wait for me to leave the car, Adam. Just sprang out and said she was heading for the nearest bus stop." He laughed mirthlessly. "I've tried getting her out every way I could, and I finally hit on the one way to do it. Just"—he made a wide gesture with his arms—"be myself." Bitter regret stabbed him like a knife, and he finished off the remainder of the whiskey in one swallow. Emma probably hated him. He hated himself and had kicked himself mentally all the way home.

"Oh, that's good. Wallow in self-pity."

Max ignored Adam's comment. He wanted to recapture the feeling he'd had, just for a moment, when he'd truly lost himself in her kiss. For that moment he had been completely unaware of anything but her lithe body pressed against him—and a flaming hunger that he had forgotten to hide.

Oh, yes, he wanted Emma Machlen.

Thunder pierced his eardrums again. He went cold. Please let her be safe, he prayed silently as he had all afternoon. The images haunted him again, images of Emma's battered and broken body lying in a rain-soaked ditch. Twisted metal wrapped her head, blood poured down her face as she lay in a bed of shattered glass.

Max groaned, and his eyes burned. If anything happened to her, he would never forgive himself.

"Don't think about it, Max," his friend ordered. "The accident happened years ago. You're safe."

"But Emma's not," he said. "You don't understand. She's out there somewhere, and it's my fault." His stomach churned with anxiety as he forced the images from his mind. "Where is she?"

"She's fine, I know she is."

"Did she call you?"

"No. But Emma has enough sense to get in out of the rain."

Max's mouth twisted. "Unlike some of us, huh?"

"Stop it! That's not what I meant, and you know it. Dammit, Max, you've just become human, here. Don't creep back into that damned shell of yours!"

"Is that what I'm doing?" He reared in his chair, his head flung back, his tawny eyes wide with worry. "I've never felt so helpless in my life."

Adam sipped his drink. He raked his fingers through his wet hair and frowned curiously at Max again. The frantic note in his voice when he'd called had been enough to send Adam rushing over. His friend's fear of the storm had shocked him, even more so when he'd found it wasn't the memory of Max's accident but fear for Emma. It was the first time he could ever remember his friend admitting to weakness, either before or after the accident. And he didn't know what to do with this unrecognizable man, especially when he liked him so much more.

Emma had affected Max more than he could possibly know.

"Are you in love with her?" he asked suddenly.

Max tensed and raised his head, his face swept with surprise. "Of course not!" he said vehemently.

Adam smiled in wonder.

"She—she's a friend. A special friend."

Adam grinned.

"Just shut up, Adam."

"I didn't say a word!"

A distant rumble of thunder followed.

"The storm's letting up," Adam said.

"Yes."

"Do you want me to leave?"

Max paused. "No." He straightened in his chair. "Thanks for coming over."

"No problem." Adam's grin widened. "That's what friends are for."

"Shut up, Adam."

Emma sprinted to the house, lifting her face happily to the drizzle. It was as if the heavens had given her a blessing, allowing the rain to stop before evening. Already the sun was making a tentative appearance. Everything would be perfect.

She slid through the front door, grinning from ear to ear, and dropped her bags on the floor. As she stripped off her dripping poncho, Adam raced through the parlor, pulling up short when he saw her. Max was right behind him. They both wore identical expressions of relief, but Emma couldn't take her eyes off Max. His golden hair looked as if he had raked his fingers through it over and over. He grasped the arched doorway the way a drowning man would grasp a lifeline. A long shudder passed through his magnificent body, and his features suddenly darkened in fury, which she ignored.

He hadn't changed his clothes from the morning, she noticed, her gaze wandering over him. Lean male hips and long legs were a deadly combination in tight jeans. He'd need to change his shirt for what she had planned. "Hi," she chirped.

"Where in the hell have you been all day?"

His voice quavered with his attempt at a reasonable tone, but she could see that his knuckles were white. "Shopping," she said, throwing a grin at Adam. His blue eyes danced.

"Why didn't you—" Frowning, he cut off the ominously building question. "Shopping?"

"I didn't come quite as prepared for all this heat as I thought. Or the rain." She laughed, shoving away the knowledge that she had spent her last dime too. If her plan didn't work, she might have to hitchhike home. It was all or nothing. "Were you worried?"

"Of course not. I—" He raked his hair. "All right, I might have been a little worried."

Adam snorted and threw Emma a telling look. She felt a pang of remorse, but squashed it as she thought of the night ahead.

Max's death grip on the doorjamb relaxed. "What would you like for dinner?" he asked calmly.

She laughed, a low, throaty sound she couldn't ever remember hearing out of her mouth. Max flushed. "Actually," she said, "I'm taking you out tonight."

"In public?" he asked hoarsely.

"Very public."

"Where are we going?"

"It's a surprise, Max. Don't you trust me?"

"Sometimes," he answered suspiciously.

"Good. This is one of those times. You'll need a different shirt. Dress casual but warmer. I'll just put these things away and . . . change."

"Into what?"

"A frog. Scoot!"

He opened his mouth to say something, but frowned instead and walked toward the stairs. He paused halfway up, turned, then gave up and finished his climb.

"What are you up to?" whispered Adam when Max was out of sight. Grinning, she turned to find his blue eyes sparkling with delight.

"You'll see," she promised.

Adam shook his head and looked at her approvingly. "Good grief! You're absolutely gorgeous."

"Thank you, sir. So are you, and you know it."

"*Moi?* Not a clue." His amusement faded. "He really was worried about you, you know. He went off the road in a storm like this, right into a tree. They had to pry the front of the car off him."

"I knew it was an accident. I didn't know it happened during a storm."

"Of course you didn't. He would never have told you." He smiled again, coaxing her with a fingertip pressed to the corner of her mouth. "Hey, don't lose whatever's driving you tonight, honey. He needs someone like you."

"I hope so." She allowed herself a tentative smile. "You're a nice man, Adam Daniels."

He sighed mournfully. "I know. It's a curse."

She couldn't help laughing.

"That's better. Now, I'll just leave you to your plans, Emma. I have a feeling I'm not needed at all." He opened the door, then paused and glanced back at her curiously. "Just what color are your eyes anyway?"

"Gray."

"They look green."

"It's a strange shade of gray." She grinned. "My mother calls it chameleon gray."

"I believe it." He shook his head. "I think I'd believe anything right about now. He's a lucky man."

"Good-bye, Adam," she said firmly, and closed the door behind him.

"Good luck," he said softly. She smiled, and her gaze wandered up the stairs to the empty landing.

Her plan had better work.

It would, she told herself, and ran into the library to call Benno and quickly outline her directions. She thought she heard a chuckle from his end, but he agreed, and she flew back into the hallway, gathering her bundles as she ran.

Once upstairs, she stripped her old jeans off and wriggled into her new ones. She changed her shirt and grabbed her new makeup. After she finished applying it, she stood back. The image in the full-length mirror made her pause for a moment.

Wide, gray-green eyes dusted lightly with green eyeshadow stared back. Her high cheekbones were emphasized by the light blush. They were framed by a stylish, short haircut that accentuated the bones of her face in a way she'd never dared hope. Her slim body was encased in skintight jeans and a T-shirt that proclaimed Go Cards!

It was like looking at a stranger, and she felt suddenly awkward, staring at herself in the mirror. For a moment her image wavered as her instincts took over, but she stuck out her tongue and left herself in full view. Confidence, Emma.

She spun on her heel and grabbed the two silky jackets from the bag on her bed before she lost her nerve. She hurried down the stairs to find Max waiting patiently beside the door, his dark glasses perched on his nose, Dixie's harness in his hands. The dog waited at his feet, as if he'd just called her in.

"You won't need Dixie," she told him breathlessly. He frowned, but returned the harness to the coat tree and reached for the cane. "Not that either."

"How—"

"You have a folding cane in the glove compartment." She transferred her bundle to one arm and reached for his hand, tugging encouragingly. "C'mon, Max. Trust me."

Instead of resisting as she half expected, Max smiled and disentangled her hand, grasping her upper arm gently. "Lead on," he said simply, and her breath caught. Something good would happen tonight. She just knew it.

Benno darted conspiratorial glances at her in the rearview mirror all the way on their silent ride downtown. He dropped them at their destination, and Max frowned as he tilted his head around, listening, she knew, to the traffic, the hollow echo, the bustling people.

"We're downtown," he said. "Emma, why are we here?"

Juggling her bundle, Emma said nothing, just shoved his folding cane and her heavy shoulder bag into his arms. "Please put that thing in my purse," she told him, unfurling the shimmering crimson jackets she carried. When he did as she requested, she retrieved her bag and draped one of the jackets over his shoulders. "Put this on. It's a bit chilly."

Frowning, he ran his hand over the satin but put it on without a word. Emma shoved her arms into hers and snapped only the bottom, blousing it artistically over her T-shirt, then fluffed the curly top of her hair forward and presented her arm to Max. "Ready?"

He nodded and took her arm. What was she up to, he wondered. They were at a curb, not far from the river—he'd heard the toot of a tugboat—but not close enough to smell it. The place was crowded, but the people were moving fast. The air smelled fresh-scrubbed from the rain, but it really wasn't chilly, even in this cool valley of concrete. Emma's whispered directions let him walk confidently across a wide expanse of cement, and it suddenly occurred to him that he had never trusted anyone enough to allow them to lead him. He ignored the implications of that and concentrated on figuring out where they were.

As they neared the crowd, Max automatically tensed for the echoes, the feeling of being trampled.

But what he heard was "The Astroturf drained fine . . . We're gonna win! . . . Kill the Dodgers. . . . Look, Steve. I wanna jacket too." And Emma's voice. "Let's lose ourselves for a while." And he knew.

Then he was jostled as they flowed into the great tide of humanity.

"Just hold on tight, Max. We'll make a break for it."

Her confident, carefree words reassured him as nothing else had ever done, but when her arm slid around his waist, he jumped. Knowing it was probably safer, he slipped his arm around her shoulders and followed her body movements, uniting their footsteps as they wended their way along.

"We made it!" she cried in relief as they reached their seats. "These people are amazing! I wanted to get here early to avoid the crowd, but"—she laughed—"they had other ideas. I'm sorry."

"Don't worry about it." He breathed deeply of the rain-washed air, letting the rumble of thousands of voices pour into him. The sharp crack of a bat echoed again and again during the pregame practice amid raucous voices shouting their commentary.

The excitement was a palpable thing, hovering over the stadium in anticipation. He had forgotten how electric a Cards baseball game could be, how the worshipping crowds felt. Some said the team actually fed on them, and he believed it. The feeling built, like a dam ready to burst, as more and more acolytes filled the temple.

The vendors circulated, their strident cries of

"Peanuts here! Beer here!" rising above the muted tide. The aroma of hot dogs and popcorn drifted on the breeze.

Emma called out to them, and then his hands were full. They ate enormous sauerkraut-smothered bratwurst, piping hot and bursting with juice, and spicy, cheesy jalapeño nachos, then washed it down with huge plastic chalices of the nectar of baseball—foamy, ice cold beer.

It was the best dinner he'd ever eaten.

The throat of the temple rose in a single, approving roar as the team reentered the playing field, and Max's heart pounded with excitement. They encouraged, applauded, lauded their gods of baseball. Max shouted his pride along with the rest, but he was somewhat disappointed because he had to depend on the crowd for the clues. Flipping up the crystal of his watch, he found to his surprise that they had been there well over an hour already, and the game was about to begin.

"Here," Emma said, shoving something into his hands. "For the game."

His hands moved over a tiny rectangular box, wires streaming like catfish whiskers away from it. Instead of barbs, though, he found earpieces at the end of the wires.

"A radio!" he cried, and fit the pieces into his ears before turning it on and tuning to the right station. Jack Buck and Mike Shannon's commentary was heard through the rumble of voices, overlaying it, clarifying without covering up.

He relaxed into his hard seat, sipping another beer, trying desperately to sort out his whirling emotions. Emma Machlen confused and delighted him more than anyone he'd ever known, and he didn't know what to do about it. He felt like a ball of yarn after the cat had gotten it, but one thing was sure. He would be forever grateful to her for this moment, a moment that captured, at least for the present, every boyhood memory of excitement he'd ever had. He didn't want to think about tomorrow, only the night ahead and the beautiful woman who sat by his side and quietly gave him the world.

"Thank you, Emma," he said warmly. "Thank you for everything." He reached out to her, running his hand up what he now knew was a crimson jacket that proclaimed them rabid fans, and cupped her cheek in his palm. "This is the nicest thing anyone's ever done for me."

"Anytime." Emma leaned into his hand, her throat burning with emotion. Unwilling to break into his excitement, she reached up and clasped his hand, squeezing gently before returning it to the arm of the seat. "Now, watch the game."

He chuckled and turned back, but Emma couldn't keep her eyes off him. His smile seemed permanently fixed to his lips, and the tawny eyes behind the edge of the glasses sparkled with little-boy anticipation. She wanted those eyes turned to her, dark and heavy-lidded, but it was neither the time nor the place.

It would happen, she promised herself silently, it would happen soon.

"Wonderful game!" Max cried exultantly as they settled into the cab's backseat. "Wonderful music! Wonderful bar! Wonderful company!" He grinned at her, the purple bruise on his cheek giving him a rakish air. He'd long since abandoned his glasses. "Wonderful, simply wonderful!"

"You sound like Lawrence Welk," Emma said with a giggle. "We should have gone home after the game," she told him sternly. "But no! You had to go dancing at some honkytonk bar." Choking back her laughter, she remembered him as they exited the stadium after the Cardinals' resounding win. Bouncing with an excess of adrenaline, nothing would induce Max to go home, and they had walked the several blocks to Laclede's Landing. Emma wished she hadn't sent Benno home, but she had to admit that the Dixieland music created a carnival atmosphere she'd enjoyed. And Max had drunk more beer.

"I couldn't sit still!" he said happily. "Too bad about the little disagreement."

"You loved that little disagreement, Max."

"He started it."

"At a different table!" She chuckled. "I turn away for ten seconds—"

"The guy was a jerk."

"I don't even know what it was about!"

"He backed down."

"Sure, after you poured beer down his leg and—"

"Can I help it if I couldn't see where I was pouring? I was aiming for his face."

"You knew exactly what you were doing. The poor guy never even knew you were blind."

"He didn't, did he?" He gave her a pleased smile.

"You're lucky he popped you only once. I would have thrown you across the room."

"You dragged me onto the dance floor before I could really get going," he said mournfully, then brightened. "You're a very good dancer."

"So are you. You didn't step on my feet at all."

"Yes, I did."

"That was the man beside us."

"Oh."

"It's okay, you apologized, hugged him, and offered to buy him a new pair of shoes."

"That was a man?"

"He was very short."

"I'm glad I didn't kiss him."

"You did."

"I did?" he groaned. "My reputation is ruined."

"I wouldn't worry about it. The guy with the beer down his leg avoided you like the plague afterward."

"Did I kiss you too?"

"Once," she said brightly. "On my eyelid."

"I think I meant to get your mouth." He frowned. "Wait a minute! Something else!" He reached for her head and ruffled his fingers through her curls. "You did something to your hair."

"I cut it. And permed the top."

"Why the change?"

"Force of habit. I've been known to change my appearance three or four times during a single conversation."

"And I thought I was dancing with Rodney Dangerfield."

"No respect," she mimicked, then laughed. "Besides, if I'm going to be with an attractive man, I want to look my best."

"I've always thought you beautiful," he told her huskily, then grinned again. "Attractive man?"

"Don't fish, Max."

"Who's fishing? How am I supposed to know? I could be wearing green pants and a purple shirt right this minute."

"You're wearing jeans, blue shirt, and a crimson jacket, and you know it."

"What about you? What are you wearing?"

Emma caught her breath. "Jeans, T-shirt."

"Please, you of all people can do better than that."

"Okay. Tight, straight-legged jeans, high-topped sneakers, a white Cardinals T-shirt, and my own red jacket."

"Thank you."

"You're welcome."

Max dropped a casual arm around her shoulders and pulled her close. Emma nestled into his companionable embrace, trying very hard to quell her wishful thinking. How would the evening end?

"Do you still have my cane?"

"Of course. In my purse."

"I used it only to go to the bathroom," he said in wonder. "I've never done that before." Shaking his head, he chuckled wryly, then kissed the top of her head. "With you, anything's possible, isn't it? It was a wonderful evening!"

"You said that before."

He chuckled again, and they were silent for the remainder of the ride. Emma couldn't speak past the lump of hope wedged tightly in her throat. His arm held her tenderly, as if she were very precious, and every once in a while he would drop a soft kiss on her head. It was too beautiful a moment to break.

The night air was chilly as the cab dropped them at Max's house, but he walked slowly in the dim moonlight, and Emma felt his reluctance to end the evening. They paused at the door, and both his arms came around her, holding her tightly. She returned his embrace fiercely, tears stinging her eyes.

Then he sighed and released her, dug into his pocket for the keys, and opened the door. Dixie greeted them joyfully, and they waited while she raced around the front yard with reckless abandon.

"She must be ready to burst," commented Emma with a laugh.

"Benno would have let her out," he said in a strange, distracted voice. "She's off duty. Questing like a normal dog."

Emma glanced up, surprised to find a tiny frown between his eyes. "What's wrong?"

"I just feel . . . different." He shook his head sharply.

"Too much beer. And spicy food. You should have a cast-iron stomach like me."

"Probably." He called Dixie, and they entered the house as the grandfather clock struck two. "Wow! I didn't realize how late it was." He turned to her awkwardly, his fair hair touched with the silvery moonlight filtering through the fan window. "Bedtime."

Emma's heart jumped, but there was nothing provocative in his statement. "Guess so."

They climbed the stairs slowly, Max one step behind her. Intensely aware of him, her body flushed with heat as she neared the top, and her heart began to race. Would he follow her to her room? Would he ask her to come to his? Was he going to kiss her?

"Emma."

His soft call halted her on the top step. She turned to find his face level with hers. His cologne wreathed her senses. Her stomach fluttered. "Yes," she whispered hoarsely.

"There's only one way to end an evening like this," he murmured.

She swayed forward until she could feel his breath caress her mouth. "Yes?"

"Only one way to make it perfect," he whispered.

"Yes?" Her lips were only a hairbreadth from his and her breasts brushed his chest. "Do it, Max," she urged gently.

She jumped back as he let out an ear-splitting Indian war whoop. Then he threw his leg over the banister and shot down the rail, landing with a thump on the polished mahogany floor at the bottom.

Before she could rush down the stairs or even cry out her concern to the vague, sprawled form, a chuckle floated up from the darkness. "Good night, Emma," he called up happily.

"Good night, Max," she called through gritted teeth. "I hope you broke your backside!"

His laughter followed her into her lonely bedroom.

Nine

Max's eyes opened suddenly. At least, he thought they did. He blinked. He was still in bed, right, he asked himself.

A sharp stinging pain in his left cheek brought him fully awake, and he touched the place experimentally. Wincing, he remembered the entire evening in a rush, and his reason for getting the bruise. The troublemaker who'd been at the next table and who'd lewdly assessed Emma should have been strung up by his thumbs, he decided ruthlessly. If he'd been sighted . . .

He sighed and rubbed his scar. What was wrong with him? How could he possibly have even considered bashing that guy's head in? How could he have lost control like that?

Tentatively he moved his legs and hissed sharply as he felt another bruise on his seat. His neck felt stiff, but his head was still in one piece. It was better than he deserved, he thought as he groaned. He'd happily lost every inhibition he'd ever had, and he almost hated himself for it. Almost.

Oddly he felt lighter, as if some weight had been lifted from his shoulders—and it scared the hell out of him. There was a part of him that was dancing to someone else's tune, to Emma's music, and he didn't like it at all. He marched to his own drummer.

His head throbbed, and he grabbed it with both hands.

"Serves you right," Emma said with a chuckle, and he immediately smelled coffee and bacon. His stomach churned violently.

"Been on the counters again, have we?" His falsely bright tone sounded strained, even to him.

"This was an emergency. I couldn't wait for you."

"You're a bad influence, you know that? You take me to some crazy places." The food odors moved closer, and as she sat on his bed he smelled eggs. He moaned.

"Don't panic," she told him softly and took his hand, pressing a small bottle against his palm. "Take a slug of this."

Max fitted the bottle to his lips, tensing expectantly for the nasty penance of some hangover home remedy. But when the potion hit his taste buds, he was surprised. "Tastes kind of minty," he said as he handed the bottle back. It didn't help, but it wasn't awful. "What's in it?"

"Shhh . . . three, two, one, now!"

His stomach convulsed once, and he gasped in agony. Then, amazingly, it settled completely. "What is that stuff?" he asked in awe. "I think it cleared my sinuses. Is it your mother's?"

"Yes."

"She'd make a great snake oil salesman. If you can survive that first jolt, it's great!"

"Mother would put a hex on me if she found out what I use it for."

"What's it supposed to cure?"

Emma stifled a giggle. "Menstrual cramps."

"What?" His face twisted in disgust.

"Max, you won't grow breasts or anything. It's a calmative, or at least it's supposed to be. Cissy was desperately hung over one morning, and I . . . experimented."

"Who is Cissy anyway?"

"Cissy is a friend. She's totally outrageous and about a hundred years old. She covers for all of us when we get in trouble. She's a writer, one of the so-called 'lost generation,' and I used to type manuscripts for her to earn money for college. Arthritis, you know. She'll be here in a couple of weeks for a charity ball."

"Her name isn't Chambers by any chance?"

"That's her."

"Good Lord, you know one of the ten best authors in this country, and you call her a writer? Have you no soul?"

"I do. Cissy doesn't."

He grimaced and rubbed his throat. "About this stuff—"

"Don't worry. Mother never puts anything even potentially harmful in her things." She touched his face, and he flinched. "Do you want some ice?"

"No." He pulled the blanket past his waist, suddenly realizing he had nothing on—and she was on his bed. Something twisted like fire inside him. He shifted, the twinge from his backside a welcome diversion from the sensations she stirred with her mere presence. Mixed with the food smells was her unique fragrance, and he halted the deep breath he was about to take to steady his reaction. It would have done anything but steady him.

He felt the pressure of a tray across his lap. The edge of something soft and silky brushed his arm. Hunger flared anew, hunger for something other than food. It quivered in the pit of his stomach, waiting.

"Plate at six o'clock," she said softly. "Orange juice at eleven, coffee at one. Toast to the left of the plate, bacon at twelve."

Max paused, stunned. "How did you know that?"

"Why do you think I was climbing your bookshelf?"

"Oh." He cleared his throat. He'd forgotten all about the manuals Shannon had purchased but never read. "Thanks."

As he ate, she watched him silently. She had tossed and turned all night, burning with images of Max making love to her. At some point she had realized what an idiot she was for getting her hopes up, but she had fooled herself into believing it could happen, that Max would jump into her bed. How could she have been so naive? He would never relinquish the reins of power so easily. Not Max. He would fight her every step of the way, and she couldn't quite understand why. He wanted to control his life, but why did that mean that she couldn't be a part of it?

Then her eyes narrowed, and she saw him as if for the first time. What exactly had happened last night, she wondered. There was something different about him this morning. The barriers were still there, but it almost seemed as if he were holding them in place instead of their being an automatic defense. Never before had she wished harder for her sister Diana's insight. She wanted to know what he was thinking, what he felt.

When she was young, she and Diana used to wander the island, searching for the small animals that inhabited it. Diana had an affinity with them and could coax them into her hand. Patience and love were a potent combination, and the tiny creatures forgot their natural instincts with Diana. Max's face held the same tentative wariness as the little animals, as if a part of him were poised for flight. But only a part of him.

She felt her nipples harden against the silk of her new nightgown as she realized what that might mean, and she breathed a silent thanks that she hadn't changed her clothes before she'd made breakfast. Patience and love.

"Emma." His soft call startled her. "I—I don't really want any more of this."

She glanced at the half-eaten breakfast. "I could heat it up."

"No." He picked up the tray and held it out to her. "Put it down, please."

Taking the tray with shaky hands, she put it on the floor and turned back to him. "Would you like anything else?" she asked, her voice a mere thread of sound.

"Yes."

Leaning up, he reached for her hand. She sat beside him, facing him, and gave it to him willingly, her breath catching as the sheet slipped to his waist. Instead of pulling her against his chest as she wanted him to, he merely fidgeted with her fingers, using both hands to stroke and fondle her as if she were a worry stone, angling his head down as if to watch the restless movement. The contact still had the power to rob her limbs of strength.

"Emma, why are you doing all of this? The game, everything."

Her heart thudded painfully, then settled back to its normal rhythm. "I wanted to understand why you were hiding."

He frowned, puzzling over her words. "I don't hide, Emma. I just don't like crowds. I don't like knowing that any moment I could trip, or run into someone, or . . . or lose myself."

"You don't like to make a fool of yourself, is that it?" Emma watched as something flickered across his face. It was gone in an instant. There was more to it than that, she thought, but he agreed with a silent nod. "Most people make fools of themselves at one time or another." She smiled lopsidedly. "Welcome to the real world, Max. Take it from the queen of fool making." She halted, her blood rushing to her face. "And I'm about to do it again."

"What?" he prompted her, reaching up to touch her gently on the cheek.

She kissed his palm. "I want you, Max. I want you so badly, I can't see straight."

"Emma—"

"And I wanted you last night, too, and I'm not ashamed of it." Her breath left her in a rush at the wonder on his face. "But the silliest thing," she went on, "is that I'm afraid you'll hurt me."

"I'll never hurt you, Emma. I swear it."

"Then you'd better kiss me soon, or I promise that I'll hide your cane and tie Dixie to a tree!"

His hand curved around the nape of her neck, and he pulled her to him, feathering exploratory kisses on her face until he found her mouth. He kissed her deeply, with a burning hunger that sent Emma's mind spinning into oblivion. His tongue plundered her mouth, searching, running over her lips until her entire body flared and her toes curled.

She leaned against him, weak with her need for him. Her hands pressed against his chest, her fingers moving restlessly over the coarse hair. She found a hard nipple and rubbed it lightly as she caught his groan in her mouth.

He grabbed her shoulders and pulled her away from him, his face swept with confusion. And passion. And something else—a heartrending, reluctant surrender. She swallowed any protest that she was about to make.

"I can't fight you anymore. You know that."

"Good," she whispered.

"I can't protect you."

"Yes, you can." She blushed. "Check the drawer in your right-hand nightstand. I put them there last night before we left."

His face darkened. "Did you think I couldn't handle it myself?"

She chuckled. "You were running from me like a jackrabbit with its tail on fire, Max. I didn't think you'd *think* of it."

"Oh." He smiled ruefully, but he still held back.

She was going to have to convince him, but it didn't seem as difficult as she'd once thought. "I'm not asking for the moon, Max."

"Just me."

"Just you." Her hand moved to his face. "Just now." She ran her fingers over his strong chin, his finely sculpted brows, traced the scar on his forehead. He shuddered and his hands loosened on her shoulders. "As much as you can give." She leaned over and pressed a kiss in the center of his chest. "No strings, no regrets." She worked her way up to his chin, touching her tongue lightly to it. "Just let me love you, Max." Her murmuring lips pressed against his. "Let me love you."

He sighed and returned her kiss gently at first, but as her mouth brushed and teased his, the kisses grew feverish in intensity. His hands slid to cradle the satin at her waist, moved back to her shoulders, and slipped the twin straps of her nightgown down. "Oh, Emma," he whispered against her mouth, "are you sure?"

Her body responded to him, swelling with startling immediacy. "I've never been this sure about anything in my life," she murmured, and kissed him again tenderly.

He bent to kiss the smooth skin of her shoulder, his breath warming her. Moist lips burned her flesh, imprinting her with his memory forever. It tore at her soul that she would leave one day, but they had the present, and that was enough. For now.

His mouth worked up toward her neck, and she tilted her head, allowing him access to her vulnerable, erotic places. He nipped the tender chord there, and she moaned softly as a tingling warmth coursed through her, flooding her with tiny golden pinpricks of sensation. He cupped her head in one hand, and without releasing his teeth's hold on her neck guided the straps completely down her arms.

A small chill struck her bared breasts, which were swollen with her arousal. His hand caressed and teased one hardened nipple. He sucked at her neck again, and sensation crashed through her body. Paralyzed with a fierce, aching desire, she was helpless as he continued his sensual assault. Every nerve ending in her body was aware of his touch.

Max groaned and let his hands roam. His hot arousal throbbed against the cool sheets, but he wanted to memorize her, taste every part of her sweet body. Her scent melted his mind, wrapping him with steamy images of pleasure. Doubts, guilt, everything but worshipping this slender body was pushed far away. He had burned for so long, but he wanted to remember the experience for the rest of his life. He wanted her to remember.

Forcing a calm he was far from feeling, he pulled back. His trembling hands pushed her nightgown to her waist, then slid higher, caressing the soft curve of her rib cage, moving over the gentle swell of breasts. Erect buds dared his exploration again, and he brushed against the sensitive nipples. Her mewing cry sent a flare into his brain, a rocket into his hammering heart. He drew her to him, bending his head to taste first one nipple, then the other. Spicy, cool, she was like a spring day, an oasis in hot sensuality.

Coherent thought flew as his tongue devastated her body. Emma tore away from him with an impatient growl and scrambled out of her nightgown, slipping between the now-warm sheets beside him, pressing the length of her body to his in a contact that only shadowed the joining she needed so much.

"I want to take this slow," he said with a groan as she pushed him back against the pillows, burying her face in his throat.

"Next time," she promised huskily, her tongue savoring the hollow. "I need you now."

"I know." He buried his fingers in her hair, tugging gently and pulling her up. She lost herself in the tawny depths of his eyes, and he brought her to him once again. "Soon."

Her mouth closed over his with subdued fury. He returned the hot demand of her lips with a fire that nearly reduced her to ashes. Rolling her swiftly, he brought her underneath him, ravaging her mouth with his tongue, liquefying the ashes. His hand moved to her breast, rolling the nipple between his fingers. Hard against her thigh, his body sent a cry of desire into her. Her love answered his growing need.

Writhing mindlessly against him, she touched him everywhere, his strong shoulders, corded neck, firm buttocks. She raked her nails across his back in a last, almost desperate urge to become one with him.

He took a hard nipple into his mouth and let his hand move lower, over the flat belly to the curly mound of hot silk at the apex of her thighs. She called out her need to him, shooting liquid heat into his loins. Still he held back, determined to give her pleasure. But when her hand closed over the pulsing shaft of his manhood, he groaned, his fragile control nearly broken. He guided her breast into his mouth again, and quickly reached into the nightstand drawer.

Emma almost cried in relief as he levered himself over her. He was driving her frantic with need. Hollow, empty, she parted her legs eagerly for him, and he entered her with a single bold thrust. Her body took his full length joyfully, uniting them in physical oneness, and she called out with the sheer pleasure of feeling him deep inside of her.

"You're so tight," he said, moaning. "So hot and so tight."

It wasn't enough. The emptiness opened again, tying her into knots of agony. "Please," she whispered. "Max, please."

He moved inside her, pulling out until she almost wept with loneliness, and she wrapped him with her legs. But he filled her again. And again. Her body moved with him, rocked with him in a single, sensual rhythm. Thrust for thrust, faster and faster they danced, until she climbed to a place past words, past thoughts, past knowing anything but him, his body, his soul. They were no longer simply woman and man, but became a tight knot of sensation that coiled, tighter and tighter, until it shattered into a blinding shower as she sobbed out his name.

Sweat beaded his brow, but he didn't pause in his feverish movement, and the knot pulled again, her need built again. She cried out as the second climax rocked her body, but this time he shuddered into her, his own triumphant cry joyfully mingled with hers.

They held each other, spent, panting, as the spasms of pleasure eased, as their single heartbeat slowed. Then he kissed her tenderly, so tenderly she ached from it, and she couldn't help the single tear that trickled down her face into the fringes of her hair. He brushed it away from her temples, and he paused as he touched the dampness.

"Emma?" he whispered, his voice hoarse with agony. "Honey, did I hurt you? I'm so sorry. I didn't know it had been so long for you." He hadn't been careful enough. Lord! She was so fragile! He'd never forgive himself if he'd caused her pain. He wouldn't allow her to regret this incredible union.

"It's not that." She chuckled breathlessly, pulling him fiercely against her. "You didn't hurt me. I didn't expect . . ."

Neither did he, he thought numbly. He grinned instead, unwilling to voice his thoughts. "You? At a loss for words? Has the sky fallen? Hell frozen over?"

"You needn't look so smug, you sod." She punched him playfully on the shoulder.

"Witch."

"Chauvinist."

His smile faded slowly. "There hasn't been anyone since your fiancé, has there?" he whispered.

"No." She sighed. "But there would have been if I'd have known—" She cleared her throat suddenly, and Max knew she was covering her true emotions again with laughter.

"Hush, sweetheart, hush," he crooned, enfolding her incredibly precious body in his arms. He kissed her temples, tasted her salty tear. He had almost touched something he'd never touched before. Some distant objective, some piece of her soul. Never had he felt another's pleasure so intensely, and he knew it was all because of her, because Emma had given him everything.

"Does it ever make you angry?"

Max drew her hand away from its restless circle-drawing on his chest and kissed her fingers. "Does what make me angry?"

"Being blind."

"Sometimes." He smiled as he realized that her soft question didn't bother him. He wanted her to understand. "I was so convinced it was temporary, even through the training they insisted I have before I left the hospital. I'd been home a few days when . . . I can't explain it, but I really thought I could see. I called my doctor and insisted on some more tests, and though he didn't want to, he did them." His fingers wandered over her face, wondering what she really looked like, but he firmly rejected any wistful, wishful thinking.

"What happened then?"

"The tests were negative, of course, and when I found out there wasn't anything in the world that could restore my sight, I spent an entire day screaming in rage and breaking things. Then I got drunk." He shrugged. "When I woke up, I was still blind, and I didn't have your mother's magic potion. I knew I could either make myself miserable or go on with my life." He sighed heavily. "I picked myself up, dusted myself off, and learned braille."

"Wasn't that part of your training?"

"Yes and no. With all the books on tape, machines to read regular print—you wouldn't believe the gadgets available—braille isn't necessary to survival." He smiled. "But being able to label your groceries, your clothes, to actually read a book instead of listen to it . . . well, I like it that way. And it doesn't bother me as much as it did then."

"And now?"

He chuckled. "Now I get frustrated only when I run into something or reach for something I thought was there and isn't, or—" His amusement fled. "Or when I make love with a beautiful woman and can't see her face."

She nestled deeper into the crook of his arm and sighed warmly against his chest. "I'm closing my eyes," she whispered. "I want to know you as you know me." Her lips brushed his nipple and it contracted, tight with a growing need that stunned him. "I want to see you as you see me."

"You—" His throat rough with tenderness, Max slid his hands along the curve of her spine as she raised herself above him and touched his face. His eyes stung with emotion. "Emma, you—"

"Shh . . . don't talk." Her fingers touched his mouth. "Just feel, Max. Feel my need for you."

"I will," he promised roughly, and captured her fingers with his tongue.

"You're not shy at all, are you?" he muttered much, much later.

She chuckled, a husky, totally satisfied sound. "Not bloody likely, mate."

His arms trembled as he held her tightly against

him. He breathed in the sweet aroma of her fragrance as it mingled with the scent of their lovemaking. It was a potently erotic combination, one he could get used to. He smiled into her hair. "You're going to wear me out, you know that?"

"I certainly hope so."

Her hand moved across his flat belly, teasing the line of hair that ran downward. Just before she reached his thighs, he groaned and captured her fingers. "Have some pity, woman."

"Nope." She struggled playfully, but he held her wrist tightly. "Spoilsport."

"What time is it?"

"I don't know and I don't care."

"I'm hungry," he told her firmly. "How about a swim before lunch?"

"Like this? In the buff? Nekkid?" She gasped in mock outrage. "What would Benno say?"

"It's his day off." Max wriggled his eyebrows. "Sound good?"

"Sounds good," she echoed, and scrambled out of bed. "Race you down," she called, her voice receding quickly.

"Unfair!" he cried. "I can't run!"

"Aw, poor baby." He heard the faint sound of her chuckle. "I guess that means I'll win a lot!"

His pride should have been stinging now, but she only made him laugh. How had he ever survived without her?

The thought chilled him, and he shoved it ruthlessly away.

"Why do you have a tree hanging over the pool? The leaves fall in."

It was usually covered, but he held on to his playful mood. He affected surprise as he let the excited Dixie out and a blast of hot air in. "There's a tree over the pool?"

"Max!"

He grabbed her bare shoulders and turned her toward him, frowning sternly while holding his laughter. "Now, Emma. You shouldn't go around telling tall tales."

"*Moi?* Tall tales?"

"I guess we'll just have to check it out ourselves." He sighed heavily and swept her up in his arms.

"Max! What are you doing?"

"Checking your story," he said, orienting himself with the sliding glass door. He began to stride toward the pool, counting his steps carefully. When he showed no signs of slowing, Emma shrieked.

"Max!"

"Now, where did I put that pool?" he mused. Ten, eleven . . .

"Max!"

His steps never faltered as he walked them straight into the cold water. "Now I remember!" he sputtered as they surfaced.

Her arms twined around his neck. "You're crazy, do you know that?"

"Shhh," he hissed against her mouth. "It's a secret."

Emma kissed him deeply, and he groaned as her tongue teased his lips. "I thought you were tired," she whispered.

"I got my second wind."

"You mean your third wind." She smiled into his mouth and his lips followed hers. "You have a smile like a ray of sunshine, Maxwell Morgan."

"So do you, Emma Machlen." His fingers touched the deep dimples on either side of her mouth, and she bit his finger. "Sharp teeth too."

She bit him again and then drew back suddenly. "I have an idea! Why don't we go to Union Station?"

"I have something better in mind, little girl," he murmured wickedly. "Would you help me with lunch?"

"I'd love to. As long as I don't have to levitate to get into your kitchen."

"Nope. Feet on the floor, the whole thing." Amazingly the thought of her in his kitchen warmed something in his heart, and his arms tightened around her. But he could sense dark clouds on the horizon. Emma Machlen embraced the world with the same wholehearted excitement she'd shown with him. And he knew he could never keep her tied to him.

But he had her. For a little while. "I think my house likes you," he said with a chuckle. "Will you stay here until the market results are in?"

"You just want someone with whom to satiate your incredible lust."

He heard the false laughter in her voice again, overlaying a breathless quality that brought tears to his eyes. He needed to keep their relationship as light as she did, otherwise he'd make an absolute idiot of himself. "Of course. Will you stay?"

She hesitated. "Do I get to do all those nasty things that have nothing to do with guests? Like laundry?"

He frowned in mock sternness. "As long as you can cook."

"My momma didn't raise no idiots," she said with a husky chuckle. "She taught me her secret fried chicken recipe. The colonel's got nothin' on us Machlens."

"Is that a yes?"

"They're due in a couple of weeks, right? I have a friend coming into town around that time." She rubbed against him. "I guess I could stay here instead of a hotel. But I don't think you know what you're getting into."

Max groaned. He knew. Oh, he knew.

Ten

The people were like mosquitoes, buzzing around them and zipping by so quickly, Max almost thought he'd imagined them. The loudspeakers echoed with demands for unknown people to come to unseen white courtesy phones. The airport smelled of leather and ink and food.

His hand tightened on Emma's arm as she guided them quickly through the crowd to Cissy's gate. He had planned on staying in the car. He really had. But somehow, after nearly two weeks alone with Emma, he was there.

A metallic, rhythmic warning beep sounded behind them. For a moment he panicked as he imagined the collision with the little golf carts they used for passengers who needed them. But Emma pulled him aside, and it passed harmlessly.

"We're here. But she's not off the plane yet."

Max sank gratefully into a chair, calming his rapid breathing. He wiped the perspiration from his brow with a nervous laugh, "It's hot in here."

"No, it isn't," she said from beside him. "Are you okay?"

"Fine." He wasn't fine, but he'd be damned if he'd let her know it. Not after he had agreed to come in with her. Why had he done such a stupid thing?

Then again, he'd been doing a lot of stupid things lately. The last two weeks had been a series of revelations, not all of them pleasant.

He'd taken her to the zoo one day. Though she'd giggled her way through the place, it had been a mistake. Not only did the crowd have its usual effect on him, but when they'd seated themselves beside a shallow duck pond, Emma had ended up smack dab in the middle of it.

His heart had jumped into his mouth as she'd shrieked. "Emma?" he'd called.

She'd surfaced, sputtering and laughing. "You pushed me!"

"I did not!" Relief dizzied him. "You just can't stay out of trouble one minute, can you?"

"The penalties of a wicked life. Don't worry, Max. I grew up on an island, remember? I'm a fish. Besides, it's as warm as bathwater."

"It's also illegal! Bathing in a public place or something. Give me your hand."

"With pleasure."

She'd taken his hand, and before he knew what had hit him, he was beside her. In the water.

Max couldn't help but laugh, yet he knew how foolish they'd both looked. And what frightened him the most was the thought of her returning to her island. He'd refused to leave the house after that.

But then again, he hadn't needed to. Two days after their first lovemaking, Emma had begun laughing over a passage in a book she was reading silently. Wanting to share her amusement, she'd read it aloud, falling into different voices for each character. Max had been so enraptured by her vivid characterizations, he'd almost seen it in his mind's eye, and he'd chuckled right along with her. Since then she'd read several books to him.

He praised her remarkable ability, but he'd nearly forgotten about it when she told him about Danny. Max swore when he heard about the man's treatment of her, his selfish abuse of her generosity. Though she laughed over it, insisted it was long forgotten, he knew it wasn't. Emma Machlen was the most beautiful soul he'd ever had the pleasure to know. "I wouldn't change you for anything in the world," he'd murmured.

"You wouldn't know you were even doing it," she'd whispered. "I can't help myself. When someone is important, their happiness is mine."

"Oh, Emma." He kissed her deeply. "I like you just the way you are. You're unique. Like—like your barometer grass. And your fragrance."

The next day when he'd returned from work, Emma had surprised him with an authentic Indian dinner. The sari she'd fashioned, the music she'd found, and the accent she'd adopted had actually transported him to the jungles of the country. After his obvious delight, on her nights to cook, he'd come home to Paris, China, Mexico, Germany, and a mythical place where they didn't wear any clothes.

She wandered the plant like a tornado, getting a remarkable amount of work accomplished on Chameleon. She'd coordinated the entire ad campaign, and he'd even offered her a job, but she'd turned him down.

She was restless. And Max felt selfish for tying her to his home.

Emma had insinuated herself into his life so firmly, he didn't know if he could ever let her go. But he'd have to, wouldn't he? She was like a breath of fresh air in his home, the house he'd once thought was the only safe place on earth, the sanctuary that was so filled with memories of her that he knew he'd never be the same when she left.

And she would leave. He knew that with certainty.

"Max, what's wrong?"

Her soft voice brought him back to reality. "Nothing." He forced a smile, but a part of him listened intently for the sounds of the surrounding crowd, for the echoes to pound into his brain until he lost all sense of direction. He heard only the powerful whine of the jets outside and the excited murmurings of waiting family members. But they would grow louder unless he could regain his balance. "Has her plane landed yet?"

"Stop avoiding the question. There's something wrong, and I want to know what it is."

"Emma, you're imagining things!"

"Max, you're brushing me off!"

He smiled, real amusement swirling through him at her playful imitation of his voice. He reached for her face, framing it in his hands. His thumbs settled in the corners of her mouth and he brought it to his, dead on target, in a quick, reassuring kiss. "Nothing's wrong. Not now."

"Is it your investment in the perfume? The market results are due in days."

He'd sensed her concern these last weeks, and he knew it was as much for him as for her family. "No, Emma, it's not that." Her worry touched him.

"But—"

He cut her off with his lips. She resisted for a moment, then relaxed into him. The realization that he would be there in the airport again with her in mere days, saying good-bye, stabbed through his heart.

His silencing kiss suddenly turned urgent, pulled from the depths of his soul.

"Max," she said, moaning.

"Shh . . ."

"Max, they're opening the door."

"What door?" His fingers threaded through her hair, and he twisted in his chair to face her.

"The door . . . mmm . . . the . . . oh, Lord . . ."

"You got one for me, too, honey?"

Max froze, the passion leaving him in a flood. That voice, that rasping, Kentucky-bourbon voice hadn't come out of Emma's throat.

"I knew about the heat wave, Emma, honey. I just didn't know it was centered here."

He felt a giggle against his mouth, and he couldn't help smiling in spite of his embarrassment as Emma broke away and turned toward the voice.

"Hello, Cissy. You have the timing of a one-piston car."

Cissy's chuckle sounded like a rusty door hinge, and it quickly turned into a cough. The sharp smell of cigarette smoke burned his nostrils.

"Why, Emma Machlen, you're still yourself!"

"Amazing, isn't it? I guess I have an indestructible core after all."

Max frowned, puzzled by her conversation, but decided it was typically Emma. Confusing.

"And who is this handsome male you were draped all over? The reluctant knight? I'm surprised he's still alive! Gracious, though, if I'd'a known he was such a looker, I'd'a sent you to London and come myself. You must be Max."

"I must be, but I'm not sure anymore." He stood and poked out his hand. "And you must be Cissy Chambers."

"Last time I checked."

His hand was taken in a surprisingly firm grip by a parchment-covered, skeletal one. She was about five feet tall, he surmised, and eighty if she was a day. She released his hand and turned to call her good-byes to the crew. An intimidating amount of fabric swished at the movement, and he wondered what kind of garment she wore. It sounded like the sail of a ship. A caftan? His mental image of Cissy Chambers caused a strangled chuckle in his throat, and the clarity of it frightened him as it danced in front of his face.

That had been happening a lot lately. Her vivid images, his lack of concentration . . .

Emma's arm came around him in a casual embrace that felt incredibly natural, infinitely comforting, though she couldn't possibly know what had just happened to him. It warmed his heart and scared him silly at the same time. What was he going to do about her?

"Yes," whispered Emma in an aside to him. "She's every bit as outrageous as you're probably thinking."

"It shows, huh?" He grinned in spite of himself. He didn't want to think about anything complicated right now. "Just tell me one thing. What color is that . . . that . . . whatever it is she's wearing?"

"Fuchsia."

Max groaned. "I knew it." He hadn't, though, and that made everything comfortably unreal.

"Shh. She's coming back." Emma giggled, then raised her voice as they began to walk to the car. "Where are we taking you, Cissy?"

"Some hotel. Don't look daggers at me, Emma-love. You know I never can remember things like that. It's the same place as that blasted charity bash I got roped into."

"Charity bash!" cried Max. "I have tickets."

"Are you going?" asked Emma hesitantly.

"If you go with me." The words were out of his mouth before he could stop them, and a wave of panic swept over him. He forced it away. What the hell? Why not?

He gave himself over to Cissy's chatter.

"Publicity! Ha! That agent of mine is going to wake up one morning even balder than usual after I snatch the rest of his hair off his head!"

"She doesn't mean that," Emma explained patiently as she automatically matched her steps to his. "Cissy and Evan have been together nearly twenty years."

"See? He's getting too old for me."

Max laughed and decided he liked Cissy. "Would you join us for dinner, Miss Chambers?"

"Cissy. Besides, technically it's Mrs. Chambers even though Lloyd skipped out on me fifty years ago."

"Don't believe her, Max. She divorced him."

"Oh, honey. Don't you go ruinin' all my good stories." The voice dropped to a whisper that sounded like fingernails on a chalkboard. "Men love women they think are safe. A husband in the background always makes for a good mystery."

"Is that a yes?"

"A yes? Oh! No, you sweet thing, thank you for askin'. But truth to tell, at my age one big event a week is enough."

"Which is why she gets along so well with her agent."

"Yep. 'Cept he can't even do once a week anymore."

Max made a strangling sound.

"Are you all right, sweet thing?" Cissy asked in concern.

"That's you, Max."

"I'm fine. I think." He shook his head. He didn't know which was worse—Cissy's bawdy humor or the fact that Emma was playing straight man for her. "We'll be happy to drop you at your hotel, Cissy. And if you change your mind, please call."

"Thank you kindly, sir, but I won't. Those are mine, honey. No, just the two. And the hat box. And the—well, aren't you just the nicest man?"

Max blinked, dazed. He had made no move toward her. He didn't even know what she was talking about. He and Emma were still joined at the hip.

"Herr Morgan? Does this . . . should I . . ."

"Thank you, Benno." The poor man sounded as confused as Max felt. "Put it all in the trunk. This is Miss—Mrs.—this is Cissy."

"Well, hello, Benno. Ooh, you're so strong. I'm

just going to sit up front and leave the lovebirds to the back, all right? We'll have ourselves a little chat."

Then they were in the car. To Max's amazement, he didn't even remember their walk through the airport at all. He had forgotten to listen. And he knew it wasn't because of Cissy's drawl.

What an idiotic moment to discover that he was in love with Emma Machlen!

Unaware of Max's stunning realization, Emma listened in amusement as Cissy's chatter and Benno's stuttered responses filled the car while they drove to the hotel. When Cissy was gone, silence settled around them like a cleansing blanket of snow. Emma curled next to Max and snuggled into the curve of his shoulder, breathing a thankful sigh of relief. Her friend always seemed to take the air out of small spaces, and it had nothing to do with cigarettes. She'd never lit one in the car. It was just her vibrant presence, or lack of it.

But Emma had to admit, Cissy had been right. Emma was a lot stronger than she had been when she'd lived with Danny. In all the years with her vocal and somewhat intimidating family, she hadn't realized she'd been protecting an indestructible core. It was only the tiny hangover from her days with Danny that kept her from declaring her feelings. Max didn't give of himself totally. Just when she thought she had him pegged he'd pull back again. But those times were few and far between these days. It's what kept her there.

She had the oddest feeling that Max was waiting for something to happen. But she didn't know what.

"It's as if you held a dove in your hand," she'd told him one night, "and were afraid to crush it. Is the world outside that dove, Max?"

"Of course not," he'd replied, and had kissed her with a passion that had rocked her. Afterward, they'd made love, and he had taken her to dizzying heights before he'd taken his own pleasure —as he always did.

She frowned. If it wasn't for her concern for his investment, these would be the happiest days of her life.

Max hadn't abused her gift of love. He'd given of himself in ways he probably didn't even realize. He'd proven himself to be the gentle, caring man she'd known was there. With patience and love, she'd show him more. She'd show him the world.

And she'd decided she would stay. Island Organics was doing fine without her. She was going to stay in St. Louis and work closely with the company that would be their exclusive buyer of barometer grass. Max just didn't know it yet.

She'd begun to drift into a comfortable doze when Max's chest suddenly shook under her cheek.

"Blanche Du Bois meets Kaiser Wilhelm," he whispered into her ear.

"What?"

"Cissy and Benno. It's all I could do to keep from saying it when she was in the car."

Emma giggled. "She grows on you. Like moss."

"I like her."

"So do I. She's been around ever since I can remember. She made me what I am today."

"A troublemaker?"

She punched his shoulder lightly. "No, Max. She taught me the importance of being yourself, even if it took me a while to learn it."

"Then I'm forever in her debt," he said gently.

Stunned by his words as much as by his serious tone of voice, Emma glanced up. Max was smiling down at her, a tender smile that warmed his eyes. Again, she had the oddest feeling that he could actually see her, that his eyes were really focused on her. But the moment passed. His smile faded.

"Max, what's the matter?"

"Nothing."

"You said that in the airport too. And I didn't believe it then either."

"It's not the same thing. I thought—never mind. Cissy confuses me."

"Cissy confuses everyone."

"Not you."

"I'm used to her."

"You're an amazing woman."

"Because I could handle Cissy?"

"Not only that. You make me forget . . . things."

"What things?"

He didn't answer right away. His arms tightened around her, and she cuddled up to him. But she frowned into his chest. "Why do you do that?" she asked softly.

"What?"

"You close up like a door, Max. Don't shut me out. It's lonely out here."

"I—" He cut himself off with a groan. "I don't want to. You have to believe that."

She was silent for a moment. Then she said, "All right. For now. But I want you to know that whatever's happening in that pointy little head of yours, it won't change anything between us."

Max's thoughts were more chaotic than she could ever imagine. His life seemed to be coming apart at the seams, yet somehow it was more complete than it had ever been. One moment he was glad she was leaving, that his life would return to normal. The next moment he felt emptiness open up inside him, emptiness that Emma filled to the brim. If this was love, he was better off with the Asian flu!

"I'm kind of glad that Cissy turned down my dinner invitation," he whispered, realizing it was true even as he said it.

"Why?"

"Because I'd like to be alone with you."

"We've been alone a long time."

He frowned, confused by the emotional volleyball going on in his mind. "It's not the same. Tonight is special."

"Why?"

"I think it's time that we talked about a few things."

"Such as?"

"Such as . . ." His voice trailed off. He really didn't know, not yet. He had to think—but quickly —because Emma would leave soon, and he knew there was a lot unfinished between them. "I don't know. I just know it's time to talk. About a lot of things."

"Why not now?"

He sighed. "Because I need a reality check."

He was grateful when she didn't press him. He had the most incredible urge to just ask her to stay with him forever. Because he was almost certain that he loved her.

But it was that "almost" that made him stop. That "almost" hadn't been there a minute earlier, not until he thought he could see her face. It had happened one too many times. Illusions. Ghosts of memory, of sight.

Was his love an illusion too? He couldn't ask her to share his life when he wasn't sure where she'd fit into it. And he certainly couldn't ask her until there was no doubt in his mind that she could. An impulsive declaration wouldn't do either of them any good, and it might hurt them both. And where would his life be if he let someone as unpredictable as Emma into it?

He would wait—and think.

Max began dinner as soon as they were home, a tiny frown playing between his brows as he worked.

Every once in a while he would pause, then shake his head as if his thoughts disturbed him. Emma held her breath on those occasions, but he did not speak to her, and she was unwilling to break in on his musings. That he was thinking about her, about them, was a near certainty in her mind. She may not get the answers she wanted, but she was sure to get something from him tonight.

Though doubt plagued her, she owed Max his solitude. She settled into the sofa, reading a newspaper to herself. She kept a pen with her and circled the items she thought Max would like to hear later. Dixie curled up at her feet and slept.

To her surprise, she dozed off too. When she awoke, luscious food odors wafted through the house. Max was still working on dinner. Had he come to her as she slept? Had he finally sorted out his thoughts? Wondering what he'd decided, she wandered to the entrance of the kitchen.

Her eyes softened as she watched him. He was so graceful in his familiar territory, more relaxed than she'd ever seen him. He poured white wine into the pot without a pause, the muscles of his shoulders bunching erotically under his tight blue shirt as he hefted the huge bottle.

Eventually she moved forward. "What's for dinner?" she asked as she entered. "It smells fantastic."

"It's a surprise. A special surprise." Smiling as if he held the secrets of the universe, he stirred the concoction and tasted a bit, then tilted his head up as he reached to the spice rack. "Did you have a nice nap?"

So he had known. "Yes."

"Do you know that you snore?"

"I do not!"

"Just a little, honest."

"Are you going to tell me what you were thinking about?"

"Later. I've come to a few decisions, but it's still a little confusing."

"That's fair, I guess."

Emma sidled up to him, kissing the point of his shoulder as he shifted and anticipated her movement to see into the pot. "I just want to see what it is," she protested with a laugh.

"A secret brew of herbs, spices, and wine."

He poured some of the spice into the palm of his hand, then dumped it in and stirred again. Something in the way he moved caught her, but she dismissed her overactive imagination. "Sounds like something my mother would cook up."

"It's Dad's recipe. He was a great chef, but was a 'pincha' cook."

"A what?"

"A 'pincha.' You know, a pincha this, a pincha that."

Emma groaned. "I don't believe you said that."

He glanced toward her, grinning, his amber eyes dancing as he leaned down to kiss her swiftly on the mouth. "You make me happy, Emma. So happy it scares me sometimes. I—I—"

He spun back to the pot, sprinkling some more of the spice into it. His words should have elated her, but Emma felt a tiny chill sweep up her spine, and she shivered. Unsettled, she dropped her hand from his shoulder and simply watched, trying to regain her joy of a moment before.

Max tasted a spoonful of his mysterious mixture, cocked his head to one side, then up as he replaced the spice and selected another one. Without running his fingers over the braille lettering, he uncapped it and shook it in. "My mother was a horrible cook," he said with a laugh. "She kept the books for my father's restaurants." He tasted again, nodded, then unerringly picked up the lid and covered the pot. "Whatever talent she lost in the kitchen she more than made up for with numbers."

He reached for the salad makings next to the

sink and picked up the knife without a falter, chopping celery quickly and professionally.

Another eerie shiver played along Emma's spine as she watched him. His head turned with the movement of his hands, and his hands never missed their targets. Emma peered into his radiant face. Her eyes widened at his animated expression, and she swallowed convulsively.

"I was pretty active," he said reminiscently. "They thought I was a changeling, I think."

"Max," she whispered, quivering.

"This poor old house rocked when I galloped through."

"Max."

"I used to play in the hidey-hole in the basement and—"

"Max!" She tugged on his arm, overwhelmed with a nameless fear.

"What?"

He turned to her, and she went cold all over. His eyes. His beautiful amber eyes were focused on her face. And it wasn't her imagination!

Her face flickered in his mind, so real, so delicate. *But he didn't know what she looked like!*

The images that danced so clearly vanished instantly, leaving him trembling and nauseated. "Lord, no," he whispered, shaking. "Not now!"

"Max? What is it? What's wrong?"

Her voice broke, but he barely heard her. "Not again," he said with a moan.

"Again?" She gasped. "You mean you couldn't really—"

He lifted a shaking hand to his eyes, pressing tightly as he fought the panic that swept him. It had been so clear!

Her voice drifted into his mind, soft, soothing in its matter-of-fact tone. "You told me that you thought you could see once, that you had gone in for some more tests. Is that what happened just now?"

He nodded wordlessly, clenching his fist at his side. His breath began to even out. It didn't matter that she knew, only that he regain his senses, orient himself again. Right now the world was a nebulous fog around him. He had to take control!

"Are you okay?"

He nodded again. Slowly the kitchen map became clear in his mind. "It's a common phenomenon, Emma, like phantom pains in a missing limb. When something's familiar, my mind remembers and gives me a clear picture, and I forget sometimes that I can't see. It's no big deal." He didn't sound convincing, even to his own ears, but dammit! He had survived this before, he could again.

"Don't tell me it's no big deal." Her hand stroked his shoulder, and it took every ounce of his self-control not to flinch away. "How often does this happen, Max?"

"Not very often . . . at least until you came." He hadn't meant to say that last part, and instantly regretted it as he heard her sharp intake of breath. "I'm sorry. I don't blame you."

"Why don't we go sit down."

"No!" He drew air deeply into his lungs. His knees were trembling, but her scent wrapped him in warmth and a strange strength that he drew on gratefully. "I don't want to move just yet, Emma, okay?"

"All right."

He felt her cheek on his back, her arms around his waist. Not pity, he realized suddenly, but one human comforting another. Emma simply could not see him in pain. Just as he had held her when she cried, so did she offer herself to him now.

Tears pricked his eyelids. Something inside him tumbled to the ground with a resounding crash.

"Emma, I—" His fist unclenched as dizzy pleasure swept over him. He loved her, and that knowledge filled his entire being. His mind lost its mental map. Lord! He had to calm down! He couldn't tell her anything with his mind in chaos. He reached out to steady himself on the counter.

Then it happened. His hand fell through into empty air. He stumbled, groping for something—anything!—as terrible, numbing fear swallowed him whole. The walls were gone, the citadel of rigid control that had protected him for so long had fallen. Sweat broke out on his brow as he battled the darkness that was more than mere absence of sight. He fought for the emotional light of moments before, for the reality, but he couldn't find it. He couldn't find it!

He knew he was moving through the house, but he didn't know where. Nothing was familiar anymore. He was lost, stifled by his fear. His breath burned his lungs, fired his throat. He had to get out of there! He couldn't let her see him like this.

"Max, no!"

He scraped his shin on something but ignored the agony in his overwhelming need to flee, to find his way back to his world.

Then he felt a touch and jerked back, repulsed by anything that would exist in this stygian darkness. His elbow hit a solid object, and the sharp pain brought tears to his eyes.

"Don't pull back from me. I love you. Let me help you."

The words floated to him, soothing him, lighting the darkness. Something warm appeared under his hand, something familiar, something safe. "Emma?" he whispered, and the fear lessened. He swallowed convulsively.

"I'm here, Max."

"Don't leave me." The grating cry was pulled from his soul.

"I won't, love. I'll never leave you."

She tugged him downward, but in his disoriented mind he saw a horrible image of tumbling into a bottomless pit. "No!"

"It's okay, Max. Trust me."

His knees buckled, and he felt himself falling, falling. Then he was on a soft, yielding object without knowing how he'd gotten there. Where was he? Nothing was as it should be!

Except Emma. He felt her arms around him, heard her crooning to him. He felt her stroke his face, which was damp, but he didn't know if her tears had wet her fingertips or his. Emma was there, she was real, not an illusion.

And she was his!

Eleven

With a guttural cry Max pulled her into his arms, holding her as if his life depended on it. He felt the blissfully familiar fire ignite, sweeping from his toes to his scalp. All of his chaotic emotions swirled to a point, focusing like an arrow into an overwhelming desire to bury himself in her, lose himself in her bright love.

He lifted her, turned his face to her breasts, ignoring her exclamation of surprise or protest while he drew her scent deeply into his lungs. His hands worked up under her blouse, restlessly exploring the curve of her spine and the satin of her skin.

"Lord, I need you," he murmured, and unclasped her bra. Sweat beaded his brow. "I need you."

Emma gasped, as much from his words as from the intense flare of desire that rose to meet his. She forgot everything that had gone before. Life started now, with a Max she didn't recognize, a driven, passionate man who no longer gently controlled the pace. It should have frightened her, but it didn't. He was ruthless in his single-minded purpose, but he would never hurt her.

Her blood pounded hot through her body, singing in her ears. He needed her! it cried. The cadence matched his murmured words over and over again, a driving rhythm that overwhelmed her.

"Don't hold back." Her voice was harsh. She buried her fingers in his hair, drawing him closer, giving him everything she had to give. She loved him, and he needed her. That was all that mattered.

He swiftly opened the first few buttons of her blouse. Emma pulled frantically at the hem of his shirt, but he shrugged her away and shoved her half-undone blouse off of her shoulders. A primal growl escaped his throat as he pulled a bared nipple into his mouth, sucking deeply.

Emma moaned in pleasure, digging her fingernails into his hair. Sharp-edged ecstasy filled her, and she wanted to shout in triumph. No more fragile doll! She felt pure, unadulterated passion, devastating in its power, beautiful because Max was giving it to her.

His arousal strained against his jeans. Her breathless moans swirled in his mind with erotic promise, exciting him to the bursting point. Never had he burned like this. He lifted her until she was on her knees beside him, shifting until he faced her. As he teased her breast with his tongue and fingers, his other hand reached up under her skirt to her panties. The thin, wispy nylon tore with his impatient pull, and he tugged the cloth away.

He shoved her skirt up and lowered her to the sofa, fumbling with his zipper as he spread her knees. With a soft rasp of metal the material parted. His imprisoned manhood throbbed at the sudden freedom, his entire body tensed with the passion that ruled him. He ruthlessly shoved his jeans and briefs to his thighs and levered himself over her.

A small part of his mind cried out. Not Emma! Not like this! Not like an animal!

But he was beyond listening. His body dominated the mind that had been so rational moments before. His entire being was centered on her, on this wonderful feeling of freedom.

His fingers dug into her buttocks as he plunged into her slick heat. Shattering sensation dizzied him, and he thrust mindlessly, lost in Emma, in the body that was made for him, in the soul that mirrored his.

A painful knot wound in his groin, tighter and tighter, until it burst. His cry of release was echoed triumphantly by Emma, and the delicious, uninhibited spasms that rocked his body seemed to last an eternity.

Gradually he returned to earth, to reality. Their rasping, uneven breathing sounded unnaturally loud in the sudden stillness. The breasts under his head were damp with perspiration, his, hers. Emma's scent mingled with the smells of their explosive joining.

His body felt suddenly leaden as a vivid picture flashed through his mind—an image of Emma lying underneath him, her clothes bunched around her waist, his own clothes still on his body.

Dear Lord, what had he done?

He began to pull up, but her arms tightened around him.

"Don't go," she whispered.

But he wouldn't listen to her, he couldn't. He had imagined her response, hadn't he? He had wanted it so badly, and it had justified his actions. Nothing could condone his shameless use of her. Nothing. He tore away, pulling his jeans up. The zipper sounded a death knoll in his ears.

"Are you all right?"

A hysterical laugh caught in his throat, and his bile rose. He had just raped her, and she wanted to know if he was all right?

"Max?"

He raked his fingers through his hair and slumped forward, his elbows on his knees. She rustled toward him, but he flinched, and she didn't touch him. He couldn't let her touch him again. He couldn't afford to lose whatever fragile hold he had on his emotions again. "I'm sorry," he said, nearly laughing aloud at the inadequacy of the words.

"It's okay. You didn't hurt me."

But I will, he thought, and a horrible suspicion insinuated itself into his mind. "Don't you dare feel sorry for me," he said before he could stop himself.

"Is that what you think? That I pity you?" She laughed, a gentle, ironic sound that wasn't funny at all. "You really are blind, aren't you?"

His mouth firmed, and he forced all his emotions deeply inside of himself. It was the only way he knew. He had to protect himself—and Emma. "Fix your clothes," he whispered.

She said nothing as soft sounds of moving fabric filled the tense air around them. Her silence was more damning than any explosion of anger. Self-loathing and disgust ravaged him, leaving him shaking. "I'm sorry," he muttered again.

"For what?"

"For . . . for what just happened."

"I'm not."

Her words would have stunned him if he had allowed them to. But he didn't. He was numb, absolutely empty inside. Nothing like this had ever happened before, and it would never happen again.

"Max," she whispered. "Don't leave me."

He hadn't moved, but he knew instinctively what she meant. But he couldn't do anything about it. He sat paralyzed by a cold knot in the pit of his stomach. He didn't want to feel anything, because then the guilt would overpower him again.

He heard his own voice but didn't recognize it. It was as flat and empty as a paper cutout. "I lost control, Emma. Completely. I couldn't control the images, I couldn't control my fear, and I couldn't control what I did to you. Do you understand? I couldn't stop myself."

"Everyone loses control, Max. It's what makes us human."

He felt her arms come around him, but it was as if it were happening to someone else, as if he stood outside of his own body. He didn't know himself anymore. "That's not human, it's animalistic. I used your body, Emma. I would have used any body that was handy." It wasn't true! "What just happened was . . . was . . ." For a moment, some unnamed emotion flickered through him.

"Important."

"No." He forced it away. "It was nothing." His hands reached out to the furniture under him. The pattern of brocade met his questing fingers. How had they gotten to the living room?

"Max—"

"I'm going to finish dinner. I'm hungry."

He stood slowly, feeling as if he were a hundred years old. Automatically he oriented himself by his now-clear mental floorplan, then walked to the kitchen, his hands helping him find obstacles he'd forgotten. It was more proof that Emma Machlen had disrupted his safe, predictable world. Something inside him died as he knew he couldn't let her stay now, and he'd have to do everything possible to make sure she left.

Emma watched him helplessly, her soul aching, her body drained. His words had hurt her more than she could ever tell him, but they were just words. He was in pain, and like a cornered animal he'd lashed out at her. But what really hurt was that she didn't know how to reach him. He'd withdrawn so deeply, she didn't know if she'd ever be able to find him again.

Dixie sat in front of her, and Emma stared at her blankly, wondering where she'd been when the fireworks had started. Not that it mattered, because Emma knew that until the harness was on, Dixie was merely another quiet presence in Max's silent house.

She glanced down at her creased clothing, damp from Max's mouth and his hurried, energetic love-making. She had been as carried away as he, reveling in his explosive passion. Didn't he understand that? It had been the first time he hadn't been so excrutiatingly careful of her, treating her as if she'd been made of glass. Emma was a woman, and for the first time she'd thought Max had realized it.

Yet he'd rejected her.

"Every time I take one step forward I get shoved back three. I love him, Dixie," she whispered, her vision blurring. Great, limpid brown eyes stared back in mute agreement. Emma reached out, burying her fingers in the soft fur, and Dixie licked her tear-salted cheek. "I just don't know what to do."

She had to try something, she thought desperately. She couldn't just let him walk away forever!

Dixie followed as Emma slipped into the kitchen. Max was hunched over the sink, rubbing his head. "Max?"

He jumped but didn't turn to her. "Please don't sneak up on me."

"I didn't sneak, I—" She bit her lip and attempted a smile. "Would you have preferred the counter?"

"I don't prefer anything. Just leave me alone."

"A little while ago you didn't want me to leave you."

"A little while ago you said you loved me."

"I told the truth." Emma held her breath, but his head dropped even lower, and he said nothing. "Did you?"

"At the time I thought it was the truth." He shrugged. "I changed my mind."

"Why?"

"I can't afford to let that happen again."

"Why?"

"You sound like a three-year-old!"

Emma couldn't let that tiny flicker of emotion she'd heard in his voice die. She ducked under his stiff arms to stand between him and the counter. He gasped but didn't turn away. "I'll stop if you will," she told him.

The corners of his mouth twitched, giving her hope, but he couldn't quite smile. "You're persistent, aren't you?"

"Yes. When it's important to me." She reached up to frame his face in her palms as he had done so many times to her. "You are very important to me."

"Emma, I—"

"I love you, Max. Before, during, and after, I love you. That's what's important." She smiled tenderly as his face seemed to soften. Her voice ached with her concern. "Please don't shut me out. Please, Max."

For a moment he leaned into her. His eyes closed, and he swallowed, his brows drawn in pain—or pleasure. His lips parted, and Emma accepted that as an invitation, leaning up to press her mouth against his. His breath blew quick on her cheek, and he yielded, just for an instant.

Then his mouth firmed. "No!" He tore away from her and backed into the next counter, grasping the edge until his knuckles were white. "Don't do that again. Don't use that against me."

"I wasn't using anything!" She curled her fingers into her hair, confused by his constant battle. "What's wrong? What are you afraid of, Max? I don't understand!"

"I'm not afraid of anything. I just don't want you here."

"I don't believe you."

"Believe it. You disrupt my life."

"You told me once that you want me just the way I am."

"An aberration. I don't now."

"Maybe your life needed disrupting. Did you ever think of that?"

"And just who are you to determine that? Who are you to judge what I need and what I don't need?"

"I'm not the one who said that! You said—" No, she thought. He seemed determined to revoke every statement he'd ever made. She straightened, and her chin came up. "What do you need, Max?"

His jaw squared. "Nothing."

"And no one?"

"No one," he echoed hollowly.

"So you want to live your life alone, unhampered by anyone who might 'disrupt' it."

"Yes."

"Won't that be rather lonely?"

"No."

She crossed her arms in front of her, eyeing him appraisingly. His posture was tense and defiant. "You're wrong."

"Emma, I'm sorry if I gave you the wrong impression these last few days. You are a wonderful lover and an entertaining companion." His voice was conciliatory, but his stiff posture told her it was difficult for him to say. It kept her from punching him.

He went on. "But you have a business to run, and so do I. I have no time for you. It was great, but it was never more than temporary."

"I thought that once," she murmured. "Now I'm not so sure."

"It's the way of the world." He shrugged. "I'd like you to go now."

"And if I say no?"

He ignored her and lifted the lid of the pot. "It's almost ready," he said. "I'm sorry you can't stay to join me."

"Don't you dare pretend I don't exist, Max."

"We bring everything on ourselves, Emma.

Haven't you figured that out yet?" He reached for the spoon and casually took a small taste. "Needs more pepper."

"I'll break in."

"I have a new security system. You know that."

Her throat burned. "I'm staying," she said stubbornly.

"Even if I don't want you to?"

"You can't make me believe that. Not after everything that's happened between us. You're running scared, and I don't understand why."

Silence stretched between them for long moments as Max carefully added pepper to the pot. When he was finished, he leaned forward against the stove, his shoulders slumped. "Do you really want to stay?" he finally asked in a strange voice that confused her even more.

"Yes," she whispered.

"Fine. You can stay as long as you like."

Her burst of happiness was short-lived as he turned to her. His face was wiped of emotion. He appeared to be a cold parody of the man she loved, and it chilled her soul.

"But it will be by my rules."

"What rules?" Her throat tightened at his ominous words. What was happening? Who was this man? She didn't even recognize him.

"No more trips to the baseball stadium," he went on in an icy voice that froze the blood in her veins. "No trips anywhere. You're here for me, whenever I n—want you. You share my bed when I want you to, but go to your room when I don't."

"Is that all?" Her voice was calm, but her heart was slowly breaking into a million pieces. It was a new tactic, but it hurt. And he knew it.

"No." He lifted his chin. "You stay out of the kitchen. No more swimming unless I say so."

"Should I write this down?" Her words had a bitter edge to them, but she couldn't help it. Her eyes blurred again, and her lip trembled. If he'd wanted to slam the door in her face, he was doing a very effective job of it.

"If you like."

"Why are you saying these things? This isn't you!"

"You're wrong. This is me. You just can't admit it."

Biting down on her lip, she forced the pain from her voice. "You really don't want me here, do you?"

For a moment she thought she saw emotion flicker on his face, but it was so quick, she must have imagined it. "No," he said. "Stability is the most important thing in my life, and if you want to stay, you have to fit into my routine. If you can't do that, then I don't want you here."

"And there is no negotiation?" This time her voice quivered, and she couldn't stop it.

He hesitated for a moment, but said, "No."

"I see." No she didn't! she thought wildly. This wasn't the Max that slid down the banister in glee. This wasn't the Max who had calmly walked them both into the pool. This wasn't the man she loved!

"You son of a bitch," she said softly. "You said you'd never hurt me."

This time she knew she saw surprise, maybe even regret in his expression. But he made no move toward her, and rage seethed in her heart, a poison in her soul. He sounded just like someone else she'd known, someone she'd thought she'd loved once. All the old, buried anger toward Danny, toward her autocratic family, focused on Max's words. "The only way I can stay is if I become your shadow. Part of the background. You want me to be a sofa. Or a window. Or a piece of the wallpaper! You want someone who won't think any of her own thoughts, who will be exactly who you want, no more, no less. You want to control me too!"

Her voice rose with each word, ending on a high-pitched squeak from her raw throat. "Well, let me tell you something, Mister I-am-the-universe Morgan. I'm not a piece of furniture. I'm a person, and so are you!" She clenched her teeth. "People . . . need . . . people. They have emotions and fears, and they occasionally lose control of their lives! And there's nothing wrong with that!"

"I—"

"You think this is stability? Dammit, Max! This isn't stability, this is stagnation!"

Tears burned her eyes, and she turned away. She bit back a sob. "I didn't feel sorry for you before, but I do now. Because the lies you're telling me are nothing compared to the lies you're telling yourself. And you're so blind, you can't see that."

She drew a deep, shuddering breath. "I'm tired of fighting you, Max. No matter how many times you let me see you—the real you—something will happen, and you'll leave me again. I'll always threaten your tidy little existence if I stay, because I would fight for you. I'd fight tooth and nail if I thought I could win. But can I ever win, Max? Can I?"

He didn't answer. Her nails bit into her palms. This was going to kill her, but it was necessary. She needed to regroup, and she couldn't do it there. Too many old emotions were mixed with the new, and somehow she knew that he would defeat her if she stayed. "You've got what you wanted. I'm leaving."

Silence stretched between them, broken only by the softly bubbling pot.

"I'll call Benno," he said finally, his voice dead of emotion. "He'll take you wherever you need to go."

"Fine."

She strode from the room before she could change her mind, but dashed her tears away and risked one quick look back. Max stood in the middle of the kitchen, chin up, his body ramrod stiff. Lord, he was so alone, her heart cried.

But he was also as approachable as an arctic wasteland, and she couldn't force herself into someone else's mold again. Not even for a little while. She'd bent enough. She would break.

"Damn you," she whispered, and left.

Twelve

"Emma, honey, you better get a move on. We'll be late."

Emma glanced over at Cissy from her cushion of pillows. Resplendent in a sequined puce caftan and matching turban, Cissy Chambers was a sight that hurt her tear-tender eyes. "I told you, I'm not going to this stupid charity thing."

She flounced over onto her side, turning her back to her friend, and stared at the twin of her own floral-printed double bed. The sharp edges of the hotel's perfectly ordered pillows blurred as her eyes filled again. She sniffed.

"Aw, don't start up again." Cissy searched for her dwindling supply of tissue with a manner that bordered on panic. "Emma, now stop that! No man is worth all this boo-hooing!"

"Stop fussing over me, Cissy. I'm fine." Emma sat up and plastered on a wavering smile. "See? Fine. You're the one running around here like a chicken with its head cut off."

"Well, hell, honey. I've never seen you cry before." Cissy sank to her bed, her turban askew, sympathetic tears filling her own brightly made-up eyes. "See? Now look what you've gone and done." She sobbed mournfully. "Now my mascara'll run right into my mouth. And at my age it's like a bunch o' little criks trailin' into the Mississippi."

Emma laughed and wiped the tears away. The wrinkles that seamed Cissy's face would surely baffle any tears that dared to fall into them. "Fix your hat."

Cissy straightened her turban, stuffing the energetic wisps of white hair bent on escape under its tight rim, then smiled, triumphant. "That's more like the Emma I know." She sat straight and rummaged in her purple handbag. She found her cigarettes, shook one out, stuck it between thin lips, and lit it with an embossed gold lighter. "Now." Exhaled smoke filled the air. "Get ready."

"Let's not go through this again, Cissy. I don't want to go anywhere."

"You want to mope."

"I'm not moping, I'm thinking." Emma forced the threatening tears back. If she started up again, Cissy would have conniptions. She'd been treating her like a contagious flu patient all day, hovering and patting her hand and tsking over the vagaries of men. Of course, Emma hadn't told her the whole story. She wasn't ready to talk about it. And she wasn't ready to write Max off yet either. She didn't know what to do, but she wasn't ready to give up on him completely.

Dammit, she should at least be allowed a couple of days to get her bearings!

Cissy, however, had other ideas. "Look, honey. You're showered, scented, and stuck. Let's not waste the first two." The concerned brown eyes suddenly turned sheepish, and she nervously flicked her ashes into an overflowing ashtray. "Besides, I . . . already called somebody."

Emma gasped. "Cissy, you wouldn't dare!"

"Oh, no, honey. Not your golden god!" Cissy dropped her gaze. "I, uh, called his friend."

"Adam?" Emma groaned. "Now, why did you go

and do something like that? How do you know him anyway?"

Cissy brightened and batted her gawdy false lashes. "Benno. He's a sucker for a lady's charms."

Emma flung herself on her pillow, burying her face in it. Not Adam, she wanted to groan. Adam was too perceptive. Adam would probably tell her she shouldn't have allowed Max to get away with it. All the things she'd been telling herself since she walked out the door the previous night.

Then again, she thought, Adam might be able to shed some light on her confusion.

"Cissy?" she called from her pillow. "I don't have a dress."

Cissy gave a rebel whoop and shot to the closet, leaving her cigarette smoldering in the ashtray. While Cissy rummaged, Emma distastefully put the thing out, wondering how the woman had managed to live so long.

When her friend emerged a moment later, turban a-kilter again, she was holding a long, shimmery emerald-green strapless gown.

"I bought it in London for Diana," Cissy said, eyeing the dress proudly. "But I think you need it more."

"I've got a bad feeling about this," Emma muttered.

Half an hour later Emma stared at her reflection disbelievingly. "Wow," she whispered.

The gown hugged every curve of her body like glittering skin. She didn't know she had so many curves! Her brown hair was swept up and spilled over the top of her head onto her high brow. Her hurried makeup job was perfect, though she looked rather puffy around her sparkling now-green eyes. Around her long neck she wore Cissy's surprisingly delicate emerald necklace. And she looked so much taller, because her high-heeled pumps were hidden by the dress that swept the floor, the length of which would be perfect on her sister.

"You look beautiful, honey," came Cissy's voice from behind her. "Absolutely lovely."

"Okay." Emma took a tiny preparatory breath. "Let go."

Cissy dropped the handful of gown she'd been holding. Emma groaned as the dress didn't fit like a second skin anymore.

"I told you! Diana is much . . . bigger than I am."

"Oh, pooh, honey. Just in the boobs." Cissy studied the fit critically, then snapped her fingers and ducked into the bathroom. When she returned brandishing a handful of tissue, Emma raised a warning hand to halt her.

"No way! I refuse to stuff myself like some Christmas goose!" Emma turned back to the mirror, glaring at the sagging bustline. She twisted this way and that, then raised her arms. The gown showed an alarming penchant for slipping down her body. Emma muttered a curse. "I can't go."

"Nonsense. Use the tissue, honey. No one will notice! I used to help your sisters all the time."

"Don't start, Cissy." Emma pursed her lips. "Do you have a needle and thread?"

"Sure, honey. This is a class place! There's a sewing kit in the bathroom." Cissy frowned skeptically. "What are you going to do? Make yourself some falsies? The tissue's easier."

"Will you stop with the falsies? I'm going to baste it up at the sides, under my arms. No one will notice my lousy stitches there, and it'll fit as snug as a bug in a rug."

Just as she finished her uneven but adequate seam, a knock sounded at the door. Emma slipped into the bathroom while Cissy answered it. Listening to Adam's drawling flattery to Cissy, she realized she missed him. And his voice brought back memories that were so new, they hurt.

"Stop it," she told herself. "There has to be a way. There has to be!"

She slid the dress over her head, but when she reached back to fasten it, the stubborn zipper told her she'd made her seams just a tad too tight. Sighing heavily, she forced the zipper up and reminded herself not to take any deep breaths. Somehow, spilling out of her dress during a swanky dinner-dance wasn't her idea of a good time.

She took a shallow, calming gasp of air and opened the bathroom door. Adam sat in one of the flower-printed overstuffed armchairs; Cissy sat in its twin. She was plying a gilt-edged puce fan with the energy of a professional flirt, and as Emma watched she playfully rapped Adam's knuckles with it. Emma rolled her eyes.

"You sweet thing," Cissy said, simpering.

"Emma!" Adam rose to his feet quickly, but he didn't throw any beseeching looks her way. Adam was made of tougher stuff than she'd thought. "You look . . . wonderful!"

"You're not so bad yourself." From the top of his perfect ebony hair, to the tips of his highly polished toes, Adam looked as if he had stepped out of the pages of a magazine. Seeing her appraisal of him, he hooked his fingers in the tux's black satin lapels and posed for her. She giggled. "You're a heartbreaker, Mr. Daniels."

"Who? Li'l ol' me?"

"I know my heart is broken, sweet thing."

"No, lady, 'tis my heart that shatters at your slightest . . . er . . . slight." Adam placed his palm on his chest and bowed to Cissy, who squealed in delight. "And now, may I escort the two loveliest ladies in the hotel up to dinner?"

"You may, sweet thing." Cissy took his arm enthusiastically, then glanced back at Emma. "C'mon honey. This is going to be a hell of a lot more fun than staring at the walls."

With a pained smile and another roll of her eyes, Emma took Adam's other arm, and they swept out the door.

Cissy chattered and Adam flattered during the ride to the restaurant-ballroom at the top of the hotel. Emma was silent, her stomach suddenly fluttering like a roomful of butterflies. When the doors swooshed open, she felt distinctly nauseated, and cursed Cissy under her breath for talking her into this.

They were greeted by a uniformed attendant who gathered their tickets and pointed them to the receiving line. The crowd was already thick in the opulent red-velvet-splashed foyer. Most of the people held glittering flutes of champagne. Emma decided she'd never seen so many sequins in one place. She felt as if she'd stepped into the pages of a Judith Krantz novel.

"Courage, Little Bit," was the reassuring whisper from Adam.

She smiled up at him gratefully, and he gave her a wink before he paraded them before the stately matron who had organized the shindig.

Within twenty minutes her face hurt from smiling. Luckily Cissy dominated every conversation. She and Adam were merely window dressing, flanking the new queen of the party. It was a role she had played before, and Emma relaxed a little. When Cissy yoo-hooed to someone across the room, Emma slipped away to a chair in the foyer, hiding behind a huge potted palm as she watched the tidelike movements of the crowd. Behind them the skyline of St. Louis went slowly by as the revolving restaurant gave everyone a view of the world around them.

The elevator swooshed open behind her, and she instinctively melted into the walls as more chattering guests arrived. The beginnings of a headache throbbed in her temples, and she wished she were at a baseball game.

•   •   •

Downstairs at that exact moment Max was wishing the same thing. The bow tie at his throat seemed to strangle him, the stiff fabric of the tuxedo rubbed his fevered skin. What he wouldn't give for a satiny Cardinals jacket and a hot bratwurst, with Emma's hand on his arm, her scent filling him with rightness. He'd loved her even then. But he hadn't been able to admit it to himself.

"The elevator is descending, Herr Morgan."

"Thank you, Benno." He cleared his throat and pulled at his tie. "When we find Emma, return to the car. Hopefully I'll be down shortly." If she accepts my apology, he thought.

"Yes, sir."

Max shifted his feet, listening to the voices around him, which were muted by the plush carpet in the lobby of the hotel. He straightened his shoulders unconsciously. He could not let his doubts defeat him. Even if he couldn't forgive his own actions, Emma would forgive him.

Wouldn't she?

Stop it! he told himself firmly. It was lack of sleep that made him so edgy, that's all. He hadn't made it to bed the night before, so torn had he been by her accusations. Lies, she'd said, and it had taken him forever to admit that she was right.

He stifled a moan for his own stupidity. How could he possibly have hurt her so badly, so deliberately? He'd broken her trust in him, and he knew just how hard that trust was to build in the first place. She was the best thing that had ever happened to him, and he was an idiot.

The elevator door opened, and he stiffened.

"To the top, Herr Morgan?"

"Yes, Benno." He stepped forward resolutely. "All the way."

•   •   •

"Here, Emma."

Adam appeared out of nowhere and handed her a glass of sparkling wine, then sat beside her. She sipped the champagne warily, deciding one glass wouldn't kill her. She wrinkled her nose at the unfamiliar and distinctly unpleasant taste.

"Your friend is amazing." He chuckled and nodded in Cissy's direction. She was holding court, surrounded by male admirers, plying her fan expertly. "Where does she get all that energy?"

Emma smiled fondly. "If I knew that, I could make a fortune."

"She wears me out." Adam glanced at his watch, then stared into his champagne before taking a swallow. "How are you doing? Really?"

Her smile faded, and she sipped again. "Fine."

"This is me, Emma. Don't snow me, okay?" He sighed. "Max looks like hell and won't even tell me what happened. Just that you'd left like he always knew you would."

She shrugged, stopping the movement as the dress tightened around her breasts. "He always knew it. I didn't."

"He won't admit how good you are for him. He's crawled into a hole and refuses to come out."

"And what am I supposed to do about that?" Tears burned her eyes, but she absolutely refused to start crying again. "He tried every way he knew to kick me out and finally hit on the one way to do it. He's very good at pushing people away."

"He's scared, Emma."

"Yes, but why? Why!"

"I don't know."

She gulped the champagne and shuddered. "That's the big question, isn't it? He's so stubborn, so damned pigheaded! Does he think he has to put on this macho act for everyone?"

"Yes, he does."

"Well, until I figure this all out, I'm not going back."

"Running away?" Adam frowned at her.

"I'm not running away, Adam. It's just a strategic retreat."

"Good. That's what I wanted to know." The elevator swooshed open again. Adam smiled his hundred-kilowatt smile, flashing perfect teeth. "He's worth it, Emma."

"I know," she whispered. She cleared her throat with a swallow of champagne and sighed. "If he would just bend a little! If he would . . ."

"What?"

"I don't know. Something. Anything!"

Adam grinned. "Would coming to the party qualify as something?"

"Maybe." Emma grimaced. "But don't hold your breath."

"I won't have to. Turn around."

Emma glanced over her shoulder and gasped at the magnificent figure standing just inside the foyer. A small pop of the seam at her side was ignored. She blinked. No, it wasn't her imagination. It was Max!

Her heartbeat raced. He took her breath away. The tux fit like a glove, and its deep blue color emphasized his golden hair. He wore no dark glasses, but he held his cane loosely over his arm as he stood stiffly, his head turning slowly as he got his bearings. Benno mimicked the movement.

Max looked lost, she thought with a wrench of her heart. And there were circles under his amber eyes, as if he hadn't slept much either. Hope filled her heart. Maybe, just maybe.

She stood and drifted to him as if she were in a dream, dizzy with the heady pleasure of seeing him again. It's only the champagne, she told herself. But she didn't believe it.

As she neared, Max's head turned toward her. Benno saw her and melted away, backing into the elevator with typical reticence. She stopped, forgetting Benno completely, wondering if she should take Max's arm or murmur some inanity or what?

He breathed deeply, and a ghost of a smile curved his beautiful mouth. "Emma?"

"Hello, Max." She shifted awkwardly from foot to foot when he didn't move. "Are you—would you—" She cleared her throat. Polite conversation wasn't her style. "Why are you here?"

"Because I—" He squared his shoulders. "The market results came in. Chameleon is a winner. They said they'd never had such an enthusiastic response before."

"I'm glad, Max." She felt the weight of a hundred years lifted from her shoulders, but it didn't ease the heaviness of her heart. "Would you like some champagne?"

"No, thank you. Is Adam here?"

"Yes, he's—" She turned back, but Adam had disappeared from his chair. "He was here a minute ago. Do you want me to find him?"

"That's okay. I—" He took a deep breath. "I wanted to talk to you."

"You could have called."

"No. Adam told me you would be here, and—"

"What?"

The elevator opened again, and a knot of people stepped around them, excusing themselves. "Is there somewhere we can go?" Max asked, tense again.

Emma took his arm and led him to the chairs. Once they were settled, he relaxed. Emma picked up her abandoned glass of champagne and finished it off in two big gulps. Her nerves needed it, she decided with a shudder.

"I missed you," Max said finally.

Her pulse leapt wildly. "Oh?"

"I—I want you to come back with me. If you still want to."

Emma lifted her chin and forced back her cry of "Yes!" She swallowed instead, controlling her voice with an effort. "That depends. Why do you want me back?"

His soft words stunned her. "Because I love you."

"Do you?" Please don't let this be a dream, she prayed. But she held herself back when she would have thrown herself into his arms.

"Yes, I do." A tentative smile curved his lips. "I thought that if I could get you out of my life, I could regain my equilibrium, and things wouldn't be so confusing. I thought I needed everything the way it had always been."

His eyes glittered. "But it didn't work. It's kind of funny. I've spent my whole life being what I wanted to be. And now it's changed. I don't know who I am anymore. But I knew within hours of your leaving that nothing would ever be the same for me. I missed your forays on my counters, I missed your scent filling my house, I missed your laughter. Hell, even Dixie misses you! The house is empty without you. Please come back to me."

She clenched her fists in an effort not to touch him. She needed more. "You hurt me."

"Emma, you know I didn't mean it. I was scared, and guilty, and very confused. I knew it would hurt you, but I couldn't seem to stop myself." He leaned over and took her hand gently in his. "Don't let me push you away."

"Is this another test, Max? Are you going to let me give you my love again, but only as long as it doesn't threaten you?" She pulled her hand from his. "How can I stop you when you do it so well?"

"Do you love me?"

"Yes." She said it quickly, surely. "But it's not enough. I don't understand you. I don't know what you want from me! We can't play a constant game of tug-of-war. I can't go through another one-sided relationship, where everything is up to me." Her voice sank to a whisper. "I just can't."

"It will be different this time," he told her. "It's

not one-sided. I love you." And she still loved him! he thought in awe. In spite of everything he'd done, she still loved him. "We can work it out."

"How?"

Max breathed deeply of her scent, his heart near bursting. It took every ounce of his courage to keep going. He had to prove how much he loved her, then she'd come back to him. "When I . . . numbed myself, after . . . after we made love the last time, I thought it was because I was afraid that if I felt anything, I would feel guilt." He swallowed convulsively. "But do you know what I felt? Loneliness. For the first time in my life I realized I wasn't complete. You were right about that. I was empty. Cold. And I'd done it to myself."

She said nothing, and Max straightened his spine. "I don't want to change you, Emma. I don't want you to be something you're not. I'm the one who should change. I'm selfish, I guess, too used to having everything my way. I won't try to keep you all to myself. You can work, or stay home, whatever you want to do. And when you get your wanderlust, you can go . . . as long as you come back to me." There! He'd said it. He'd admitted that he needed her in his life, that it wasn't one-sided. It was the most difficult admission he'd ever made.

"What do you mean, as long as you come back to me?"

Confusion swamped him. Her tone was disbelieving. What had he said? "I was obsessive, stifling. I mean, I won't try to stop you when you want to go."

"You could go with me."

"No, honey, I can't. I have absolutely no desire to go wandering with you." He smiled, leaning over to frame her face in his hands. "But that doesn't mean you can't go anywhere you want."

"You came here."

"Because I had to." He frowned. "Emma, don't you understand? I want you to share my life."

"But you don't want to share mine."

"I can't!"

"Why?"

"Because—" He groped for words but none came. What was happening?

"You don't have a reason, do you?" She tore her face from his grasp, and he made no move to stop her. "Tell yourself the truth for once! You're so pigheaded, Maxwell Morgan."

"Morgans aren't pigheaded, Emma. Machlens are!" He raked his fingers through his hair. "A Morgan is self-reliant, a Morgan is persistent, but—"

"A Morgan is a horse, Max! Why won't you let me in! You're putting me firmly outside your life again, don't you understand that?" She growled, low in her throat, sounding just like a fox threatened with a gun. "You're impossible, do you know that? That's all I am to you, isn't it? A crutch! I don't know what to do about you!"

Her voice trailed off, and Max began to panic. She was walking away from him! "Where are you going?"

"To get some champagne."

"You don't drink!"

"I just started!"

Then her voice was gone.

Thirteen

Emma searched, without much success, for a waiter carrying champagne. Excusing herself constantly as she wended her way through the crowd, she was just about to admit defeat when she was flagged by Cissy. With a quick glance back in Max's direction, which was useless because of the thick crowd, she heeded the summons and slipped to Cissy's side.

"Where's Max?" she called over the ever-increasing din.

"Back by the elevators. The sod." Emma flounced into a velvet chair and felt another tiny pop at her side. "Great," she muttered. "I'd better fix this dress before June comes bustin' out all over."

"Trouble in paradise, honey?"

"Yes." She glanced to her bodice. It wasn't to the critical point yet, and she could breathe easier. If the remaining stitches held, she'd be safe. "He's the biggest pain in the neck since Dracula."

"So are all men, honey." Cissy sat back and sipped from a huge glass of something pink. "Want to talk about it?"

"No. I'm just looking for a couple of stray glasses of champagne. I think both Max and I need something to calm ourselves before we strangle each other."

Cissy chuckled. "I haven't seen you this riled since the day Marshall beheaded all your dolls."

"Who's Marshall?" asked Adam from behind them.

"My brother." Emma grimaced. "And Max is just about to go the way of Marie Antoinette."

"I don't think decapitation will change him all that much, honey."

"Oh, Cissy, I don't want to change him. I just want him to listen to reason!"

"Whose reason, Emma?"

Startled, Emma stared at her friend with wide eyes. "I never thought of it that way."

"Seems to me," Cissy said as she lit another cigarette, "that Dracula has company at this party."

"He's isolated himself, Cissy. I want to let him be a part of the world instead of apart from it. Is that wrong?"

"You tell me."

Emma frowned. Something flickered in her mind, just out of sight.

Cissy blew a plume of smoke. "I remember a ten-year-old girl who swam a couple of miles through barracuda-infested waters because she couldn't live with everyone tellin' her what to do."

"You did that?" asked Adam with admiring eyes.

"And yet that same little girl hadn't believed in herself enough to let the man she loved see her in all her mischievous glory, simply because it wasn't what he wanted."

"Cissy, if self-confidence was a prize, Max would win the Nobel."

Cissy's eyes narrowed. "And that same little girl found out she could let the world see what it expects, because fooling people into a false security was easier than fightin' for domination. It was survival."

"Emma," Adam said gently. "Max has always been this way. Don't let him get to you."

"He told me about his parents, Adam. They wanted him to be like them, like . . ."

Her eyes narrowed. Max's voice echoed in her mind. "A changeling," he'd called himself. The events of the previous evening, the last weeks, flashed before her too. She had seen only Max's loss of control. But if she shifted the perspective . . .

She gasped. She'd forgotten something elemental, something she'd known after their first argument. If Max's control was *protection*, like her illusions, then that would mean . . .

"I have to find him!"

Cissy grinned. "Sharp as a tack, that girl."

"I think I missed something," Adam muttered.

Emma picked up her skirts and pushed through the crowd. No more strategic retreats, she told herself firmly. She would drag him out of there and lock him in his library if she had to, but they would settle this in private.

Max was a better illusionist than she ever was. His sightlessness had distracted her away from the real trouble. She'd concentrated so much on understanding him that she'd missed something vital.

Max trusted her. But he didn't trust *himself*.

Benno would help her, she knew. She and Max were going to settle this once and for all! There had to be a compromise, and he had made the first move. What they had was worth fighting for, even if she had to fight Max or herself to get it.

But when she rounded the potted palm, she stopped dead in her tracks. Max was gone.

Max paused when he ran out of wall. It had taken every ounce of self-control he possessed to get this far, and he wasn't sure he could continue. Damn Emma, anyway, for wandering off before they'd had a chance to finish their talk.

The polite murmur of voices washed around him. Though he had been greeted several times, there seemed to be no more acquaintances in his immediate vicinity, and he was grateful for that. He had to find Emma.

Max listened intently to the voices. He heard the guffaw that he knew belonged to one of his father's oldest friends. He heard the shrill laughter of someone he used to date. The clink of glasses intermingled with the swish of heavy fabric. The cloying scents of mixed perfumes floated around him, and the smell of beef, probably prime rib, heralded the entrance to the banquet hall.

He'd gone too far. He'd been aiming for the ballroom. And there was only one way to get there now. Straight through the crowd to the other side.

His heart lurched at the thought.

He clenched his sweaty fingers around the solid cane. It was his fault, and he owed it to Emma to explain. He didn't want to cage her, she was the flip side of his own personality, the freer side. She was everything he hadn't been for so many years. Through her he saw the world again, and he didn't want to lose that.

With a deep, steadying breath, he plunged into the sea of faceless bodies.

As the first person jostled him with murmured apologies, Max stiffened. Music began, a soft waltz, and his head swiveled in its direction. The ballroom. His breathing evened out now that he had a definite direction. He held his cane to his side so as not to skewer anyone and took another hesitant step in the right direction.

Another jostle. Another apology. Another greeting that he acknowledged with a patently false smile. Another pause to wipe his palm down his jacket.

He wasn't going to make it, he thought in rising panic. The room spun in his mind, the music floated from all directions, louder and more metallic with every dissonant note. His pulse jumped with every sound, every touch. The mixture of scents was a stifling blanket that suffocated him.

He remembered another crowd, a tide of worshipping baseball maniacs. They hadn't confused him. With Emma at his side, he hadn't felt horror. She made everything so easy.

He froze at the thought. Dear Lord, she was right. He'd used her as a crutch. He'd caged himself with gilded, self-imposed bars of supposed control. He'd vicariously seen the world through her eyes, but he hadn't bothered to try to see it himself.

That's what she had tried to tell him. All along she had led him not to relinquish control but to regain it! His illusion of a safe world was just that. An illusion. A fleeting attempt to create a cocoon and shut out reality.

The voices around him flowed like a gentle stream. The scents resolved into individual fragrances. The jostling creatures of his nightmares were just people. He was merely another among them.

A marvelous feeling of freedom swept over him. The air around him felt rarefied, as if he stood on top of a mountain he had been climbing for years and found a beautiful valley nestled in the snow.

Without Emma it was colorless. But it was there!

"Max!"

He turned at Adam's voice, a bright, real smile on his face. "Adam, where's Emma?"

"She went looking for you twenty minutes ago."

His smile slipped. "She didn't find me."

"Obviously. What happened? Why were you grinning like that?"

"Tell you later. Do you see her anywhere?"

"No. I've been looking for her. She's not here at all." Adam snapped his fingers. "She said something about her dress. She had to repair her dress."

Max took Adam's arm easily. "Would you take me to the elevator? I don't want to waste any time."

"Sure."

Max chuckled at the surprise in Adam's voice as they began a fast pace. "I've been walking in circles all night, I think. And it's my own fault. Benno's waiting in the lobby, so don't expect either of us back, okay?"

"What if she's not in her room?"

"Then I'll just have to figure out another way to get her back. If I have to fly to South Carolina or Timbuktu, I'll do it. Dammit, I'm not dead yet!"

Adam left him at the elevator in stunned silence, and Max grinned.

Emma flew into the lobby, halting only when she saw Benno. She breathed a hearty sigh of relief. Max couldn't have gone home without his chauffeur.

Grabbing her slipping bodice, she paced carefully over the plush blue carpet. Benno saw her and blinked. Then he smiled. Emma raised her hand in greeting as he hurried toward her.

"Has Mr. Morgan come down yet?" she asked, breathless.

"No. He told me to wait, that he wouldn't be long." He grinned. "He went to find you, I think."

"He found me, Benno. But we're not finished yet. I need your help." She tugged at her dress and bit her lip. "Do you think you can smuggle me out of here?"

"*Ja*, I think so. The car is right out there." He handed her the keys. "You sit in the front, okay?"

"Okay." She winked. "Thanks."

Emma hurried out of the hotel into the humid

night. The car was in front of the building as Benno had promised, and she slipped the key into the lock. She climbed into the front passenger seat, unlocked all the other doors, and settled down to wait.

Her heart fluttered as she envisioned the confrontation to come.

A muted bellow startled her, and she glanced up to see Max storm from the hotel. Benno scurried in front of him, barely opening the door in time.

One look at Max's face told her she'd better wait until they were home before she opened her mouth. Benno threw her a speaking glance and started the car. She scrunched down in the seat, trying to make herself even more invisible to him.

The car pulled away, and she began to relax—and to plan. Max's new security system was dismissed as unimportant. She would figure something out. She always did. It would go like grease through a goose, she thought with a smug grin.

"Benno," Max grumbled from the back, "do we have mice in the car too?"

Emma swallowed convulsively and peeped over the seat. Max sat with his legs casually crossed, his head cocked to one side, his golden brows raised in faint inquiry. No, she thought. He couldn't possibly . . .

"I hope you're not planning to break into my house," he commented blandly. "You know it won't be so easy if I prosecute. The judge won't drop the charges."

She grinned. "It'll work out. It always does, Max. Always."

"I know that, Emma." He cocked his lovely, tawny head. "Do you know when I first fell in love with you?"

"The baseball game?"

He smiled gently. "I thought that too. But you know what? I was wrong. I fell in love with Emma

Machlen . . ." He cleared his throat. "I fell in love with you the moment you entered my house and turned my predictable world upside down."

Tears blurred her eyes. "Max—"

"Even then I knew you were something special. But I don't want a crutch, Emma. I don't need one."

"You never did," she whispered.

"But you know what I do need? A partner."

She caught her breath. "You're just saying that to get my barometer grass essence."

He grinned. "That too. What do you think? Can Island Organics and Daniels Cosmetics come to some reasonable compromise? Do you think a merger is in order?"

"I think we can arrange something." She clutched at the bosom of her dress. "But I want more."

His voice dropped to a husky purr. "Then climb over."

She glanced over to Benno, who pointedly turned the rearview mirror toward the ceiling and turned his attention toward the road. Grinning, Emma began to slither over the seat. The last of her stitches gave way with a loud pop, and she grabbed her dress with both hands, losing her precarious balance. With a tiny shriek she twisted her body and landed with a thump on the floor. "Damnation," she said, wondering if she'd ever be able to do anything right around him.

"You sure know how to make an entrance," Max said.

"It's a gift," she agreed solemnly, shifting to rub her backside.

"Want me to kiss it and make it better?"

Her mouth worked, but she lost the battle when she turned to find Max grinning at her. She giggled. "Do you happen to know what you're offering?"

"I think so." He wedged his body beside her on the floorboard, touching her gently on the side, then slid his hand down the silky gown until he cupped her injured muscle. "Here?"

"Yes," she whispered. "But, Max—"

"Hmm?" He caressed her buttock and leaned to nuzzle her neck, no easy task on the floor of a moving car.

"You're kneeling on my foot."

He chuckled and moved to the seat, reaching down to help her up. She put her hand in his. The dress slipped as she rose. When she instinctively snatched at it, Max's hand came with hers and brushed against her revealed breast.

He froze. "Is this a new style?" he murmured, running his fingers lightly over her.

Breathing became an unnecessary function. "I think I need a safety pin. I—"

Max leaned to capture her mouth in his. Emma wound her arms tightly around her neck as he lifted her to his lap without breaking the kiss. He trailed light kisses down her neck to her exposed breast, and drew it deeply into his mouth while Emma moaned and pulled him closer, feeling herself flow away, melting into the man she loved. They were one in their passion.

Then Max froze, chuckling breathlessly. "I think we'd better stop before Benno has a heart attack," he whispered.

"Stop is not in my vocabulary right now," she whispered back.

"What about marriage?"

"I know that one."

"Good. Emma, will you marry me?"

"Yes. Let's discuss it later." She kissed him again, but Max chuckled against her mouth, and she drew back, grinning into his face. "What?"

"Just yes?" He pulled her to the cradle of his throat. "No 'But Max, won't our lives go to hell in a handbasket over the next fifty years?' "

She laughed at his choice of words. "I think we

can manage. If you talk to me. But," she warned him softly, "our life won't be perfect. I'm stubborn."

"So am I," he whispered.

"And I love baseball."

He chuckled into her hair. "So do I, love."

"We're going to fight."

"I wouldn't love you so much if you were afraid of offending me." He pulled her fiercely against him. "I don't want to control you."

"About that." She hesitated. "Max, will that happen again?"

He tensed. "The phantom sight? Yes. What happened afterward? No."

"I hope you're joking."

"Emma, it happens occasionally, but I won't shut you out again. At least I'll try not to."

"Good. But about the afterward part . . ." She tilted her head up and framed his face with her hands, guiding it down to her. "I'm not shy," she said against his mouth. "And I'm not made of glass." She pressed her lips against his, delving deeply into his mouth with her tongue.

She felt him swell against her, heard his moan of desire, and she reveled in her power. He swallowed convulsively as her lips drew away. "What are you, Emma Machlen?"

"I'm a woman, Max. And I love you."

"I love you, you little witch. You were made just for me."

"And you me." She pulled back and gazed into his face. "Do you trust me?"

"Implicitly."

"Then there are a few things we still have to get settled."

"Such as?"

"It's about control, Max. There are times when control doesn't matter one damn bit."

He grinned, and her spirits soared. "Convince me later," he murmured huskily. "We have something to do first."

"If it's a baseball game, I'll pass."

Max threw his head back and laughed as she'd never heard him laugh before, holding her tightly against him. "No, not a baseball game. Something better."

"That sounds promising," she said, and nibbled his neck.

"Oh, it is," he answered, his face shining with love for her. "Benno!" he called. "Take us to the nearest amusement park, and step on it!" His smile softened. "I have a feeling I'm in for the roller-coaster ride of my life."

"Depend on it," Emma muttered.

THE EDITOR'S CORNER

What an extraordinary sextet of heroes we have for you next month! And the heroines are wonderful, too, but who's paying all that much attention when there are such fantastic men around?

Iris Johansen is back with a vibrantly emotional, truly thrilling romance, **MAGNIFICENT FOLLY**, LOVESWEPT #342. Iris's man of the month is Andrew Ramsey. (Remember him? Surprised to reencounter him as a hero? Well, he is a marvelous—no, magnificent—one!) When this handsome, unusually talented, and sensitive man appears in Lily Deslin's life, she almost goes into shock. The intuitive stranger attracts her wildly, while almost scaring her to death. Abruptly, Lily learns that Andrew has played a very special, very intimate role in her life and, having appeared as if by magic, is on the scene to protect her and her beloved daughter Cassie. Before the danger from the outside world begins, Lily is already in trouble because Andrew is unleashing in her powerful emotions and a deep secret she's kept buried for years. Iris's **GOLDEN CLASSIC, THE TRUSTWORTHY RED-HEAD**, is now on sale. If you read it—and we hope you will—we believe you'll have an especially wonderful time with **MAGNIFICENT FOLLY**, as Andrew, Lily, and Cassie take you back to Alex Ben Rashid's Sedikhan.

Ivan Rasmussen is one of the most gorgeous and dashing heroes ever . . . and you won't want to miss his love story in Janet Evanovich's **IVAN TAKES A WIFE**, LOVESWEPT #343. The fun begins when Stephanie Lowe substitutes for her cousin as cook on board Ivan's windjammer cruise in Maine coastal waters. Descended from a pirate, Ivan sweeps Stephanie off her feet while laughing at her Calamity Jane performance in his galley. He had never thought of settling down until he embraced Stephanie, and she had never been made to feel cherished until Ivan teased and flirted with her. But Stephanie has her hands full—a house that's falling apart, a shrivelling bank account, and some *very* strange goings-on that keep her and Ivan jumping once they're back on terra firma. There is a teenager in this story who is an absolutely priceless character as far as those of us on the LOVESWEPT staff are concerned. We hope you enjoy

(continued)

her and her remarkable role in this affair as much as we did. Full of humor and passion, **IVAN TAKES A WIFE** is a real winner!

Imagine meeting a red-bearded giant of a man who has muscles like boulders and a touch as gentle as rose petals. If you can dream him up, then you have a fair picture of Joker Vandergriff, Sandra Chastain's hero in **JOKER'S WILD,** LOVESWEPT #344. We can only thank Sandra for taking us in this story back to delightful Lizard Rock, with its magical hot springs and its wonderful people, where Joker is determined to heal the injuries of former Olympic skater Allison Josey. He mesmerizes her into accepting his massages, his tender touches, his sweet concern . . . his scorching kisses. Her wounds are emotional as well as physical, and they run deep. Joker has to fight her demons with all his considerable power. Then, in a dramatic twist, the tables turn and Joker has to learn to accept Allison's gift of love. As heartwarming as it is exciting, **JOKER'S WILD** leaves you feeling that all is more than right with the world.

Rugged, virile, smart, good-looking—that's Nick Jordan, hero of the intense and warm romance **TIGRESS,** LOVESWEPT #345, by Charlotte Hughes. What a dreamboat this sexy peach farmer is . . . and what a steamy delight is his romance with Natalie Courtland, a woman he finds stranded on his property during a freak snowstorm. The cabin fever they come to share has nothing to do with going stir-crazy as the storm keeps them confined to his home; it has everything to do with the wild attraction between them. Beyond their desire for each other, though, they seem to have nothing in common. Natalie is a divorce lawyer in Atlanta, and Nick has forsaken the world of glamorous condos, designer clothes, sophisticated entertainment, for a way of life he considers more real, more meaningful. How they resolve their differences so that love triumphs will keep you on the edge of your chair. A true delight first to last!

Ooh, la, la, here comes Mr. Tall, Dark, and Handsome himself—Dutton McHugh, Joan Elliott Pickart's devastating hero of **SWEET BLISS,** LOVESWEPT #346. When Bliss Barton wakes up with her first ever hangover, she finds a half-naked hunk in her bed! She could die of

(continued)

mortification—especially when she recognizes him as one of her brother's rowdy buddies. Dutton is not her type at all. Careful, cautious, an outsider in her family of free spirits, Bliss has kept her wild oats tightly packed away—while Dutton has scattered his to the four winds. When her family misunderstands the relationship between Bliss and Dutton, and applauds what they imagine is going on, Bliss decides to make it real. The hilarious and touching romance that follows is a true joy to read!

Fayrene Preston outdoes herself in creating her hero in **AMETHYST MIST,** LOVESWEPT #347. Brady McCullough is the epitome of rugged masculinity, sex appeal, and mystery. When Marissa Berryman literally falls into his life, he undergoes a sudden and dramatic change. He is wild to possess her ... not just for a night, but for all time. The confirmed bachelor, the ultimate loner has met his fate. And Marissa, who goes up in flames at his touch, is sure she's found her home at last. Parted by the legacies of their pasts, they have to make great personal journeys of understanding and change to fulfill their destiny to love. A breathlessly exciting love story with all of Fayrene's wonderfully evocative writing in full evidence!

I reminded you about Iris's **GOLDEN CLASSIC,** but don't forget the three other marvelous reissues now on sale ... **SOMETHING DIFFERENT,** by Kay Hooper; **THAT OLD FEELING,** by Fayrene Preston; and **TEMPORARY ANGEL,** by Billie Green. What fabulous romance reading. Enjoy!

With every good wish,

Carolyn Nichols

Carolyn Nichols
Editor
LOVESWEPT
Bantam Books
666 Fifth Avenue
New York, NY 10103